# LAW

# MAN

★

G·K
Hall
&Cº.

*Also by Lee Leighton*
*in Large Print:*

Beyond the Pass

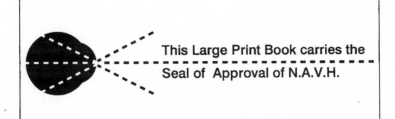

This Large Print Book carries the
Seal of Approval of N.A.V.H.

# LAW
# MAN

## LEE LEIGHTON

G.K. Hall & Co. • Thorndike, Maine

Published in 2000 by arrangement with Golden West Literary Agency.

G.K. Hall Large Print Western Series.

The text of this Large Print edition is unabridged.
Other aspects of the book may vary from the original edition.

Set in 16 pt. Plantin.

Printed in the United States on permanent paper.

**Library of Congress Cataloging-in-Publication Data**

Leighton, Lee, 1906–
    Law man / Lee Leighton.
      p.  cm.
    ISBN 0-7838-9273-X (lg. print : hc : alk. paper)
    1. Sheriffs — Fiction.  2. Large type books.  I. Title.
PS3529.V33 L45  2000
  813′.54—dc21                  00-061429

# LAW

# MAN

# Chapter One

**ON** Friday the fifteenth of June, the sun rose early, coming up between the twin peaks of Red Mountain so that the first sharp light fell directly on Bill Worden's face. He woke with a start, moving his head on the pillow, and his first thought was: *This is the morning.* He knew at once it wasn't. He had to wait another twenty-four hours.

Worden had been sheriff of Grant County for eleven years. His term had another year to run. But he wasn't concerned about what would happen during that year. He wasn't concerned about anything except tomorrow. It was like a high wall; he couldn't see over it or around it. In the morning he would hang Ed Lake.

He turned his head so he could see his wife's face. It was a pretty face, serene now in the peace of sleep. In a country with hard water and a devastating, dry wind and a sun that hammered at the earth from May through September, a woman's beauty usually faded like the transient glory of a desert flower. Somehow Ada had retained hers.

Her hair lay in a dark brown mass on the pillow. She was breathing easily, her lips lightly parted. Her ability to sleep, regardless of the pressures and fatigue of the previous day, always amazed Worden, but it was typical of her, and without quite understanding how it was, he knew that he received much of his strength from her.

They had been married twenty-one years. A good marriage. Worden could not have asked anything more from life than he had received. She had not protested when he first decided to run for sheriff. If she worried when the duties of his office brought him into danger, she gave him no hint of it. She had a simple faith that he could handle any situation that came up. He always had, but she didn't understand about tomorrow.

The sun was in his eyes again, and Worden moved to the edge of the bed and stared at the ceiling, still dark with night shadow. No, she didn't understand this business about Ed Lake. He didn't understand all of it himself. There was much that had not come out at the trial, much that would probably never come out.

His thoughts turned to George Ballard. Many of the people of Grant County expected Ballard to get Lake off. There was no evidence that Ballard had anything to do with Lake's coming to Grant County, or with the murder Lake had committed, but the belief prevailed that Ballard would do something for him.

Ada had not indicated she knew anything about it, and Worden hadn't told her. He was sure their daughter Ellen didn't know, either. She was engaged to Ballard, the wedding date set for early July. Ever since Lake's trial, Worden had been haunted by the feeling that he should stop the wedding, but he didn't know how to do it, so he had done nothing.

A restlessness began working in him. He had no reason to get up at this hour, but he couldn't lie here in bed without waking Ada and she needed her sleep. Carefully he laid back the blanket that they had pulled up sometime during the night and slid out of bed. He picked up his clothes and gunbelt, gently pulled the door shut behind him, and crossed the living room to the kitchen.

He touched a match to the fire he had laid the night before, filled the tea kettle at the pump in the corner of the kitchen, and set it on the front of the stove. He dressed slowly and made coffee, listening absentmindedly to the pitch pine crackle in the stove, and he wondered who was really guilty of the Smith boy's murder, the man who pulled the trigger, or the man who had hired the trigger pulled, if there had been such a man.

He sighed. A decision like that was not his to make. He had done all he could. The water in the tea kettle was hot now, and Worden poured some into a pan and, carrying it to the table, began to shave in front of the mirror that hung on the wall. He was nervous, so nervous that he cut himself three times before he was done.

After he finished, he stood by the fire and drank two cups of coffee. He considered fixing breakfast and decided against it. He'd eat at the

Chinaman's later in the day. Funny thing how a man's fear worked, he thought. Lake was a dangerous man. Worden had known that when he'd arrested him, but he had not been afraid. He was afraid now, though. A different fear, but it was fear just the same.

It was a tribute to Worden's integrity that he had been elected sheriff three times in a county that was torn between stockmen and farmers, a county where violence threatened every Saturday night. It would threaten again tomorrow morning when he hung Ed Lake.

Most lawmen took pride in their gun skill or in acts of courage. Bill Worden dismissed things like that as being simply part of his fitness for office. The way he saw it, a man had no business taking a sheriff's star if he wasn't handy with a gun, or if he lacked the physical courage it took to do the tasks that were his to do.

Bill Worden's pride was rooted in the fact that both the stockmen and farmers had trusted him for years. Now he was losing that trust. He understood exactly what the situation was and it hurt him.

The farmers said he was failing in his duty because he had not arrested the man who was responsible for Ed Lake's coming to Grant County and shooting the Smith boy. Two men had been murdered before young Smith, probably by Lake, the farmers said. They were convinced that Ballard had hired Lake and should have been tried for murder, too. But no, Worden hadn't touched him. And why? Because his daughter was going to marry Ballard. It was that simple.

Worden buckled his gunbelt around him. He put on his coat and hat, and walked into the living room. He paused there, wondering if Ada was awake and wanting to talk to her if she was. But, listening, he heard no sound that indicated she was up, and moved to the door.

He paused again, eyes on the stairs. He had built the house just before he was elected sheriff. Ada had drawn the plans, with two bedrooms upstairs for the children. They had been small then. Now the boy, Kirby, almost nineteen, was working for a big outfit on the other side of Red Mountain. He would never be home to stay. Ellen, twenty, would be married next month and she'd be gone.

There had been a time when he'd been able to talk to Ellen. She had wanted him to put her to bed when she was little and she had liked to have him sit beside her and read before she went to sleep. Now it seemed a long time ago. As she had grown up, she had drawn apart from him.

He wanted to go upstairs and wake her and talk to her as he had when she'd been a girl, to ask her if she really loved Ballard, or was it something else that would sound ugly if he put it into words? Ballard was Gunlock's banker and the owner of the biggest ranch in Grant County, the one man who could give her the luxuries it was natural for a woman to want.

11

Ballard was thirty-two, twelve years older than Ellen. He had been engaged to Nan Laren when she had operated the Stockman's Café, but they had broken up two years ago and she'd married Lew Hogan, a little rancher who lived far up Coffin Creek where it spilled down from the foothills. She had taken Hogan on the rebound, so the gossips said. About that time Ballard had started going with Ellen.

Worden went outside, carefully closing the front door. No, he couldn't talk to Ellen. He couldn't even talk to Ada about it. She'd say, "Why, Bill, there's nothing wrong with George. They've been engaged for months. What in the world are you getting upset about it now for?" And what could he say to that?

He paused on the porch long enough to fill and light his pipe. There wasn't a single thing he could put his finger on to prove that George Ballard had anything to do with the murders, not a single thing he could cite for proof that Ballard was unworthy of his daughter. Maybe his feeling was due to the fear that the farmer-talk would spread until it shadowed his own reputation. If that was true, well, it made him a pretty small man.

He walked down the hill toward Main Street. The early morning air still held the night chill. The town was asleep, with only here and there a column of smoke rising from a chimney to indicate that someone was getting breakfast.

He passed Doc Quinn's house. Barton, the

12

storekeeper's place. Judge Webb's house, the man who had sentenced Lake to death. Worden stopped, and turning, looked back at Ballard's fine house farther up on the hill, the biggest in Gunlock. The lawn surrounded by a metal fence, the cast-iron deer in the yard that was too heavy for the kids to steal at Halloween, the mansard roof, the stained-glass door.

Worden pulled on his pipe, wondering if Ellen would be happy once she had moved there. He had been a lawman so long that it was difficult to think about family problems, but now he chewed on his pipestem, and the restlessness that had touched him when the sun had first wakened him began gnawing at him again.

What would he do if Ballard abused Ellen? Or if he was unfaithful to her? Nothing, he thought sourly, as long as he was sheriff. But if he was a private citizen, he'd beat hell out of Ballard. Or kill him.

Swearing softly, Worden swung around and walked rapidly toward Main Street, his long shadow leaping beside him. He remembered the day Ed Lake had ridden into town. Worden had just finished eating dinner in the hotel dining room with his deputy, Mike McNamara. Mac had stopped him as they'd left the lobby.

"Take a look, Bill," Mac said. "Is there a circus coming to town?"

Lake looked like a circus performer, all right. A green silk shirt with pearl buttons, a white Stetson that had probably cost fifty dollars or more, and a gold-plated gun in a fine, hand-tooled holster. He was riding a black gelding, a fast animal judging by his trim body and long legs.

Lake was a big man, and when he pulled over to the walk and stepped down, he stood a good three inches taller than Worden, and a full head above McNamara. He said, "Howdy, Sheriff. You've got a good-looking town here."

"We like it," Worden said.

Lake tied his horse and stepped up on the walk beside Worden, glancing briefly at McNamara and bringing his gaze back to Worden. "How are the beds in the hotel? And the grub?"

"Good." Worden disliked Lake at once. Perhaps it was because of his showy clothes, or more likely his face, square and muscle-ridged with heavy brows above his dark eyes and a meaty-lipped mouth. A brutal man, Worden decided, and added quickly, "I'd ride on, was I you, mister. You won't find a job anywhere in the valley."

Lake laughed. Worden heard that laugh many times afterwards, a rumble that came from far down inside Lake. His lips held the look of laughter long after the sound was gone, but it didn't reach beyond his mouth. His eyes were cold and faintly calculating as if measuring the toughness in the lawman who stood before him.

"Was I asking for a job, Sheriff?" Lake shook his head. "No sir, I ain't no thirty-a-month cow-hand. When I like a town, I stay. When I don't, I move on." He nodded, and went into the hotel.

As Worden turned down the walk toward the courthouse, McNamara said softly, "He won't stay in Gunlock. Just a showcase, Bill. You see that gun? By God, it was gold-plated."

That had been almost a year ago. Two months later a farmer who had taken a claim on the north side of Coffin Creek was shot in the back. They found him with his hat over his face, a rock as big as a man's fist holding the hat in place. Within a week the farmer's family left the county, and his quarter section was swallowed by Ballard's Lazy B. The creek was the boundary, the stockmen said. The country to the north was going to stay in grass.

Late in the fall another man settled on the wrong side of the creek, a bachelor just up from Colorado, driving a covered wagon with a plow tied on the side. Getting married in the spring, he said, after he had a house built and a crop in. Just after the first snow he was found beside his wagon, a bullet in his back, his hat on his face, a rock on the hat.

Both times Worden and McNamara went over the ground carefully as they could, but there were no clues. A delegation of farmers led by Preacher Rigdon called on Worden. Rigdon said, "There's ten thousand acres of good farm land north of the creek. Ballard can't keep it from being plowed if he murders a dozen men, but what we want to know is how long you're going to let him go on murdering."

15

McNamara had blown up. He was red-headed and Irish, and always short-tempered, and he worshipped Bill Worden. He yelled, "If you think we're sitting on our butts and letting these men get murdered . . ."

Worden got him by the shoulder and shook him. He said, "Shut up, Mac." Then he looked squarely at the preacher. "Do you know who's responsible for these murders?"

"I say it's Ballard," the preacher said without hesitation. "He's the leader of the ranchers. Of course it could be Lew Hogan. Or Jess Ryman. They've both made some tough talk about what would happen if any of us crossed the creek."

"I've talked to all three of them," Worden said. "They can prove where they were the nights the murders were committed. Now if you have any evidence that points to the killer, it's your duty to tell me and I'll arrest him."

That was the end of it for a time. Even now Worden wasn't sure anyone had suspected Lake. He was usually in town, gambling in the Casino, or occasionally riding around the country on his black gelding looking for a ranch to buy. Apparently he had some money. At least he was lucky at poker, and Worden, who had checked with the bartender in the Casino, judged that Lake had won two thousand dollars or more.

Worden privately queried Lake about where he'd been when the two men were murdered. The man was indignant, which was natural enough, but he'd finally said he'd been out at

16

Hogan's place one night, and the second time he'd been on the other side of Red Mountain. He'd spent the night in a line cabin with a cowboy named Knut Jensen. Both of his alibis stood up, although now Worden was convinced that both Hogan and Jensen had lied.

The third time was a case of the pitcher going too often to the well. It was March, a couple of inches of snow still on the ground. A family named Smith had spent the winter in town. There were four grown boys and a father in the family, and although they knew about the murders, they decided they could handle anything that came up; they took land north of the creek.

Within three days the youngest boy was shot. When Lake appeared from the brush, the boy's father rode over a ridge and recognized the killer. They traded shots, but Lake got away and the father headed for town to get Worden.

Lake almost made it out of the country. He struck out for the state line, but it was rough going, and his black gelding gave out on him. He was on foot when Worden and McNamara caught up with him.

He claimed he hadn't done it, but the day was cold and the frozen snow retained his tracks. Worden went out there with Lake's boots, taking George Ballard and Doc Quinn along as witnesses. There was no doubt about who made the tracks.

Now as he moved down the street to the courthouse, Worden thought about all that had happened, and how Ballard had testified at the trial about Lake's boots fitting the tracks. The jury, mostly townsmen, found Lake guilty and Judge Webb sentenced him to hang.

After that the talk had started about Ballard. Farmer-talk, but the townspeople had picked it up. There was another rumor that worried Worden. The stockmen were going to break Lake out of jail. For a week now, and probably still today, a man could go into the Casino and get even odds that Lake would not hang.

Worden climbed the stairs in the courthouse to his office. He took off his coat and hat and hung them up, then walked along the hall to the jail. McNamara slept on a cot in a small office that had no other furniture except a desk and a gunrack. He had spent every night here since the trial except for a few times when Worden had spelled him off so he could have some fun in the Casino.

McNamara was getting up when Worden came in. He yawned and rubbed his freckled face. "You're up early, Bill," he said.

"A little," Worden agreed. "Any trouble?"

"Not none." The deputy pulled on his boots, looking up at Worden. "Lake wanted to make me a bet he'd be out of here by sunup tomorrow."

"How big a bet?"

"A thousand dollars," McNamara said. "As if I had it."

"Go get your breakfast. Fetch some for Lake, too."

McNamara put on his coat, still a little sleepy. He yawned loudly, then he said, "What do you figure they'll do?"

"Nothing."

"Hell, you're just wishing," McNamara said, and left.

Worden unlocked the heavy iron door that led into the corridor and walked back to Lake's cell. He was the only prisoner, and Worden was thankful for that. He looked through the bars. Lake lay on his bunk, apparently asleep.

For a moment Worden stood there, staring at the man. There was nothing about Lake now that made Worden think of a circus performer. Here, in this tiny cell, Lake had no opportunity to show off, no room to strut. Still, after all these weeks, he had not broken.

To Worden's way of thinking, a back-shooting, hired killer was a coward at heart who would reach for any straw to save himself. This was the part of Lake's makeup Worden could not understand. The fellow was as defiant as he had been from the first, admitting nothing, blaming no one. Perhaps he still expected to be freed, even now with time running out. Or it may have been he had his own peculiar code of honor that kept him from naming the man or men who had brought him here. Either way, Worden was forced to admit that Ed Lake had his share of courage.

"Lake," Worden called.

The man stirred and sat up. "What the hell?" he grumbled. "Still night, ain't it?"

"Not quite," Worden said. "What do you want for supper?"

Lake rubbed his face and yawned. He dropped his big hands to his sides and stared at Worden, black eyes filled with the feral wildness of a forest animal. Once again the thought came to Worden that Ed Lake must have killed for the sheer love of killing, and not for any money he might have expected to receive.

"Chicken 'n dumplings," Lake said finally. "How about getting it from the hotel? The grub you've been fetching me ain't fit for a hog."

"All right," Worden said. "Lake, you're hanging tomorrow. Why don't you clear up those other two killings?"

"Don't know nothing about 'em."

"Why did you come here?"

"Just happened to ride in. I've told you that fifty times."

"You're lying."

Lake got up and came to the bars. He shouted, "God damn you, Worden, get out and leave me alone. Someday I'm coming back to kill you."

"You can't come back if you don't get out." Worden gripped the bars, his face close to Lake's. "Who paid you for that killing? Was it Ballard?"

Lake gave him the deep, ugly laugh that he hated. "You wouldn't believe it if I said it was

Ballard. It'd bust up your gal's marriage."

Worden whirled and walked out. He locked the heavy door and moved to the window. He stood there staring down at the gallows that had been finished only yesterday, and he wondered whether he would believe it if Lake named Ballard. And what would it do to Ellen if he did?

Worden turned away, suddenly aware that he was sweating. More than twenty-four hours to wait. He wasn't sure he could.

# Chapter Two

**BY** Gunlock's standards, George Ballard habitually woke up late and went to work late. There was no need for him to live any other way. He never worried about the Lazy B, for his foreman, Jiggs Larribee, was a better cowman than Ballard, and there was no question about his loyalty.

Ballard had no worry about the bank, either. The cashier, Timothy Brown, was as good a banker as Jiggs Larribee was a cowman. He could be depended upon to open the bank precisely at nine, to wait on the customers and adroitly postpone any important decisions until Ballard arrived, and to watch over the bank's money and reputation with the anxiety of a clucking hen mothering a flock of chickens.

The use of men like Larribee and Brown was largely responsible for Ballard's success. Others, like Lew Hogan and Bill Worden, were manipulated with far more finesse than Larribee and Brown. They never dreamed that Ballard was using them at all. If they had been told, the teller would have been promptly knocked flat on his back. It was in keeping with Ballard's character that he found far more satisfaction in this kind of intrigue than in anything else he did.

22

Ballard mentally took credit for pawning Nan Laren off on Lew Hogan. And as for Ellen Worden, that was one of the shrewdest moves he had ever made. She was pretty enough and she would be the gracious hostess he needed when he had important visitors from the capital. But more important was the fact that she was Bill Worden's daughter, and Worden was one man who successfully walked the tightrope between the farmers and the stockmen.

On the morning of the fifteenth Ballard woke earlier than usual. He couldn't blame the sun, for he always closed the heavy drapes at his windows. It was, he knew, the business about Ed Lake.

Ballard's worry had grown since the trial. It simply wasn't natural for the man to keep his mouth closed, now that he had barely twenty-four hours to live. Not that Lake had any proof Ballard had paid him for the killings. Lake didn't need proof. All he had to do was to name Ballard.

Now Ballard lay in bed and went over in his mind what had happened. He had no regrets about anything, for it had been and still was a matter of survival, and every cowman north of Coffin Creek knew it as well as Ballard.

There had been a time when Grant County did not have a single farmer. Ballard's grandfather, old Longhorn, had brought the first cattle to the valley when buffalo herds were on the grass and Indian tepees were a common sight near the creek just below town. Others had come, men like Doc Quinn and Judge Webb who were young then and old now, all of them ranchers or at least friendly to them.

For almost two generations, there had been no trouble in Grant County except Indian scares and an occasional case of rustling. Ballard's father started the bank. Zane Hosmer built a livery stable. Judge Webb set up a law office. Tad Barton built the false-fronted structure that housed his Mercantile and stocked its shelves.

George Ballard grew up in that era, and he looked back upon it with the nostalgia that invariably marks man's memory of "the good old days." Stories of violence, such as the Johnson County War, were heard in Gunlock and dismissed lightly. Nothing like that would ever come to Coffin Creek Valley.

Ballard's grandfather died, then his father, and he inherited both the Lazy B and the bank. By the time he was twenty-five, he was the most important man in the valley. But the era passed and the farmers came, the first colony led by a hellfire-and-brimstone parson known as Preacher Rigdon.

They settled south of the creek because irrigation was no great problem there. The outfits in that area were greasy sack spreads, for it was hard-scrabble range, and there was no organization, so the transition was made without violence. Some of the ranchers left the county, some moved to town, and the rest went to work on the bigger spreads north of the creek or beyond Red Mountain.

Ballard watched it happen with misgivings. This was the backwash of the homesteader movement, finally reaching Grant County because the good land was taken elsewhere. It took no omniscient powers on Ballard's part to see that the invasion had not run its course. Already the government had forced the stockmen to take down their fences on public domain, further proof that the "good old days" were gone. In other parts of the country ranchers who had used fraudulent means to secure title to their range were being sent to prison.

Realizing that power lay in union, Ballard called a meeting in his home of the stockmen north of the creek, and the Grant County Cattlemen's Association was formed, with George Ballard president. They posted signs that read, "No homesteaders allowed north of Coffin Creek" and for a time the bluff worked, but Ballard wasn't lulled into complacency.

Sooner or later someone would call the bluff, and with Bill Worden wearing the sheriff's star, it was stupid to think that the cowmen could run the invaders back across the creek. Violence of that nature would have worked in Ballard's grandfather's day, or even his father's. Now it wasn't even to be tried.

Not quite a year had passed since Ballard had had a private talk with Lew Hogan. In Ballard's opinion, Lew wasn't very bright. But he was a hard worker, making something out of nothing far up on Coffin Creek, starting with his two hands and a few hundred dollars he saved from his cowpuncher wages on the Lazy B. Very likely Lew had used a running iron, but like many men who were a little on the dull side, he had a native shrewdness that instinctively warned him about how far he could go.

Hogan had other characteristics that suited Ballard's purpose. He was fiercely loyal to Ballard who had given him work when he'd needed it after Jiggs Larribee said they had more men than they could afford. Too, and this was the part of Hogan's nature that suited Ballard, he had a moral standard that would not balk at murder if the survival of his ranch was at stake.

All men took pride in something. With Lew Hogan it was his wife Nan and his Circle B, and they went together. He couldn't go back to punching cows and support Nan; and so when Ballard planted his seed, Lew took the subtle suggestion without knowing he was taking it.

A few days after his talk with Hogan, Ballard called a meeting of the cattlemen's association. Hogan was there. Marv Tremaine of Skull, Jess Ryman from Rocking Chair, and most of the others. Ballard laid it on the line and they listened.

"We might as well face facts," Ballard said. "We're using range we don't own. If we lose it, we're finished. The law says the farmers can come in and fence our grass and turn the sod and steal our water. The way I see it, the boys south of the creek lost out because they were short on guts and they weren't working together. We don't have those weaknesses, but I'll admit I'm at a loss to know just what course of action we should take."

Jess Ryman, by nature a violent man, said, "I can tell you, Mr. Ballard. There's still guns to be hired. Hell, we'll put riders on the creek with orders to shoot the first man who drives across with his wagon and plow."

Marv Tremaine, lacking the toughness of the others, said, "And we'll wind up in the pen, or with a rope on our necks."

"We've got to face it," Ballard told them. "We have three choices, none of them good. We wait and let the settlers move onto our grass. Or we take Jess' suggestion and set Bill Worden on our tails. Or . . ." He stopped, studying the men before him. Then he shook his head. "No, I guess we don't have three choices. We just have two."

That was when the seed he had planted in Lew Hogan produced a crop. Hogan jumped up, red in the face from the anger that had been building in him. "I don't care what the law says, Mr. Ballard. There is such a thing as justice, and it ain't justice for these sons-of-bitches to steal everything we've got."

Tremaine asked, "Got a suggestion, Lew?"

"You bet I have," Hogan shot back. "Mr.

27

Chairman, I want to make a motion, but first we've got to agree to keep this out of the minutes and we've likewise got to agree not to open our mouths to nobody."

Tremaine rose. "If this ain't in the open, I'll have no part of it."

He started toward the door, but he had not taken three steps before Hogan had a gun on him. He said, "Marv, this is sink or swim. We hang together, or as the fellow says, we'll hang separately. You're with us or against us. Which is it?"

Tremaine looked at the gun in Hogan's hand; he looked at Ballard and saw no encouragement there, then he turned to Ryman. "Jess, last year you wanted to buy me out. That still go?"

"I'm a mite short on cash," Ryman said.

"Your credit is good at the bank," Ballard said.

Ryman's sun-weathered face broke into a grin. "Thanks, Mr. Ballard. Marv, I'll see you in Judge Webb's office at ten in the morning."

"I'll be there," Tremaine said, and left the house.

"What's your motion, Lew?" Ballard asked.

"I move that we throw five hundred dollars apiece into the kitty," Hogan said. "There's nine of us here. That makes forty-five hundred. One of us takes the money and hires an outsider. We don't know him. He don't know us. We get hold of him by mail. We pay him a thousand dollars for every sodbuster who gets plugged after he

28

settles on our side of the creek. My idea is that after one or two of 'em get it in the brisket, they'll stay where they belong."

Ballard looked properly shocked. So did the rest of them, even Jess Ryman. There was a murmur of protest, then Hogan shouted defiantly, "All right, what else can we do? We hang rustlers and horse thieves, don't we? Why shouldn't we take care of a bastard who steals our grass?"

Hogan was smart, Ballard admitted, in taking that point of view, smarter than he had expected him to be. Then Ryman said in a low voice, "I second the motion."

It was passed without a dissenting vote. Ballard said, "I'll tear up a sheet of paper. I'll mark one piece and leave the others blank. Whoever gets the marked one will make the necessary arrangements. We'll leave the money on the table. I'll blow out the lamp and we'll circle the table three times. The man who gets the marked paper will take the money, but the rest of us will not know who it is."

He had thought this out before the meeting, knowing that only by some such method could the man be protected who would be responsible for the killings that were bound to follow. From the first he had intended to be that man.

Ballard tore up a sheet of paper and pretended to mark one of the fragments, then he mixed them up and they drew. He noted with amusement that all of them were frankly relieved when they discovered they had drawn blank slips of paper.

They put the money on the table, mostly in greenbacks. Several of the men — Lew Hogan was one — did not have five hundred dollars in their pockets, so Ballard loaned them as much as they needed. He dropped the money into a sack, blew the lamp out and then, in the absolute blackness, they circled the table three times.

Ballard picked up the sack the second time around and slipped it into his pocket, having no worry about being detected. All of their hands were on the rim of the round table, guiding them, so it was impossible for the others to catch the slight movement of Ballard's hand from the edge of the table to the sack of money and back again.

After they left, he laughed silently, pleased with the way it had gone. He trusted no one but himself. They were bound to question each other, and all would deny drawing the marked slip of paper, but no one would believe anyone else.

Ballard had heard of Ed Lake and his reputation. He wrote to the man at once, printing the note in pencil so that Lake could not identify him by his handwriting. The note read: "You will be paid one thousand dollars for the removal of each settler who takes up land north of Coffin Creek in Grant County. Don't try to contact anyone when you come to Gunlock. The money will be mailed to you. To establish that you have earned the money, leave the subject's hat over his face and lay a rock on the hat."

Ten days from the time Ballard mailed the letter, Ed Lake rode into town. Ballard had started home for dinner when he saw Lake stop in front of the hotel and talk to Worden and McNamara. It was the kind of cool effrontery that Ballard liked. He frowned as he went up the hill, surprised at Lake's appearance. He had never seen the man before, but he had no doubt about his identity. Strangers seldom came to Gunlock.

Lake was big and good looking in an ugly way. Ballard smiled at the thought, but it was true. Lake's features were rough: a fat nose and a thick-lipped mouth and black eyes that had the glitter of chipped obsidian. Still, in the short moment he had looked at Lake, he had been attracted to him. Ballard didn't like the showy clothes, but Lake undoubtedly knew what he was doing. In the cattle country people were inclined to take a man like that lightly.

In the days that followed Lake made a reputation as a gambler. The gossips said he didn't intend to buy a ranch at all, that he was a card shark who pretended to be a cowman. Although he made few friends in the valley, no real friends except Lew Hogan, he never had trouble finding someone to play with. Once he had established his reputation, there was a certain excitement in playing with him, and it was not uncommon for the older, more sedate citizens like Doc Quinn or Judge Webb to sit in on a game that ran until well after midnight.

Ballard dutifully paid off after the first two killings. Then, one dark night in February, Lake called at Ballard's house. He said, "Don't worry. No one saw me come. I want to talk to you."

Ballard's housekeeper had gone to bed. Although there was no one else in the house, Ballard was vaguely worried. He said, "If you're looking for a private game, I suppose I can accommodate you. Shall we say Saturday night?"

Lake sat down without waiting for an invitation. He laughed and winked at Ballard. An odd laugh that always worried Ballard when he heard it, a deep sound that was a sort of rumble. Lake's lips curled at the corners, his cold, brittle gaze seemed to probe Ballard's soul, and the uneasiness in him grew. He wasn't exactly afraid of Lake, but he didn't want him here.

"I don't want any more poker than I'm getting, Mr. Ballard." Lake leaned back in the Morris chair and lighted an expensive cigar. "It's a funny thing about men like you. Rich and high and mighty. Always looking out for your reputation. Law-abiding as hell." He blew a smoke ring toward the ceiling. "You all run to the same pattern."

"I don't know what you're talking about," Ballard said.

Lake grabbed the cigar out of his mouth. "You damned mealy-mouthed hypocrite, I'll bet you go down to Preacher Rigdon's church every Wednesday night and lead the prayer meeting. I'm doing your dirty work for you, so don't put on that pious face in front of me. Maybe you ain't paying me. I dunno. Might be Lew Hogan. Or Jess Ryman. Or one of the others. But you know about it, all right."

Ballard shrugged and dropped down on the leather couch. It was a cold night with snow on the ground, and Ballard had a roaring fire in the fireplace. Now he shivered, a prickle working along his spine as he looked at Lake. No one could prove anything against him. But, as Lake had said, he was careful about his reputation, and Lake could start talk.

"What is it I'm supposed to know?" Ballard asked.

Lake muttered something obscene. "I came here for one thing and I'll make it plain. This sheriff you've got is a pretty smart hombre. He keeps digging. Might be my luck will run out. Well, you're the big boss in this town. If I'm arrested, it's up to you to get me off. Savvy?"

"I still don't have the slightest idea . . ."

"Oh hell." Lake got up and clapped his Stetson on his head. "Just remember what I said, or you'll be right up there with me."

He slammed out of the room. For a long time Ballard didn't move. He had been very careful, so careful that he was sure Lake could do nothing but point to him, and pointing was not enough to drag a man like George Ballard down.

33

Still, it was far better not to be pointed at in the first place.

After that Ballard grew steadily more nervous. He'd heard some of the whispers, probably started by Preacher Rigdon and the farmers. He would have been far wiser to have sold the Lazy B and been content with the bank. But he was not a man to waste his time regretting a past mistake.

After Lake was arrested for the Smith boy's murder, Ballard mailed him the money. He slipped a note into the envelope, printed in pencil the same as the first letter had been. He simply said, "You'll be convicted, but you won't hang unless you try to implicate someone else." That the jury would bring in a verdict of guilty was a foregone conclusion. Weeks ago Judge Webb had pronounced sentence. Lake was to hang on the morning of the sixteenth of June. That was tomorrow. So far Ballard had done nothing.

Now, staring at the shadowy ceiling of his bedroom, Ballard wondered what would happen in the next twenty-four hours. Twice within the past week Hogan had been to see him. "What are we going to do, Mr. Ballard?" Hogan had asked. "He's our man. We owe him something, a jail break if that's the best we can do."

"It's his worry," Ballard said. "He let himself get caught."

But Hogan with his peculiar standard of morals didn't see it that way. Whereas Ballard

34

wanted Lake to hang so his mouth would be shut forever, Lew Hogan felt a crazy sense of obligation.

Ballard's thoughts were broken into by a knock on his door. He called, "What is it?" His housekeeper asked, "Are you sick, Mr. Ballard?"

"No, I just overslept," Ballard said. "I'll be right down."

"I'll have your breakfast ready," the woman said, and went back downstairs.

Ballard rose and dressed, realizing it would have looked better if he had gone to the bank at the usual hour. He shaved hastily, trying to make up time, and for once finding no pride in his bathroom, the only one in Gunlock that had hot water piped to the wash basin and tub.

A few minutes later he left the house, dressed as usual in his tailored black broadcloth and wearing his expensive black Stetson. He always dressed conservatively as befitted a man who was both banker and stockman. Part of the game was to hold the respect of the ranchers and townsmen. He cared nothing for the farmers and had little business with them.

For some reason he felt a strong desire to stop at Bill Worden's house and see Ellen. It was not the thing to do, and he wondered with some concern why he had this urge to see her. But he knew. She loved him and she trusted him, and through these last weeks as time had run out, he had discovered that she was good for him. He had never before doubted his ability to handle any situation, but he did now, and just being with Ellen helped to restore his confidence.

x As he turned along Main Street he met Doc Quinn hurrying to his office. Doc was one of the old timers in the valley, one of the few who had been part of what Ballard mentally termed "the good old days." Doc had been a friend of Ballard's father and grandfather, and for that reason he felt a benevolent interest in Ballard.

Doc stopped and tipped back his once-black derby, now a sort of bottle-green. He said, "Well, George, you figure Bill Worden's going to get Lake hung in the morning?"

Ballard was irritated, but he hid it behind a ready smile. "Bill Worden usually does what he sets out to do."

Doc nodded and looked up and down the empty street. Then he said in a low tone, "George, there's a lot of talk running around that the cattlemen's association will get him out of jail. Know anything about it?"

"Not a damned thing. Should I?"

"You're president of the association," Doc said tartly. "Now you listen to me, George. I don't know what to believe, but one thing's sure. Lake was sent for and paid for them killings. Might've been the association. Might've been you personally. Or some of the others."

Ballard was angry and it took no effort for him to sound angry. "That's pretty hard talk, Doc. All I know is it wasn't me and it wasn't the association."

36

"All right, all right," Doc said as if he didn't believe it. "But I'm telling you this and you'd better listen. Let the bastard hang and don't you make a move to stop it."

Quinn stomped on down the street. Ballard went on to the bank, mentally counting the hours until Lake was dead. It would be better if someone could get to him today, but that was impossible, up there on the second floor of the courthouse and guarded by Bill Worden or Mike McNamara.

He had another shock when he stepped into the bank. Jeannie Mason was sitting in a chair waiting for him. Of all the people in town, Jeannie was the last one he wanted to see. She was in love with Lake, a pathetic, stupid love that Ballard did not understand. It was common gossip that she had been living with Lake, and the strange part of it was that she'd had a good reputation before Lake had come to town, almost too good.

Ballard took off his hat. He said, "Good morning, Jeannie."

She was a plain woman in her early twenties who made a living as a dressmaker, or had until the talk had started about her and Lake. She said, her pale lips unsmiling, "I want to talk to you privately, Mr. Ballard."

If she got him alone, she'd cry on his shoulder and he couldn't stand that, not this morning. He shook his head. "I'm sorry. I don't have time."

"Then I'll say it here." Jeannie glanced at

Timothy Brown who was sitting on a high stool working on a ledger. Apparently he wasn't listening, but Ballard knew that he was. Jeannie said in a low tone, "You've got to help Ed."

"I owe him nothing," Ballard said. "The law must take its course."

He stalked past her to his private office behind the bank. When he glanced back, he saw that she was standing there, crying as he knew she would. Damn a weepy woman! He paced around his office, smoking a cigar before he reached a decision.

Lake would talk if someone didn't make a move to help him. But Ballard could not afford to go to Jeannie and work out a jail-break scheme with her. Still, she was the one because she'd do anything for Lake.

Jess Ryman? No, he was too inclined to jump in head first. Lew Hogan? Sure, he was the logical choice, but again there was too much risk in going directly to him. It was then that Ballard thought of Hogan's wife Nan. There had been a time when she would do anything for him. Perhaps her feelings had not changed. At least he could work on her greed.

Ballard left the bank at once, and getting his team and buggy from the livery stable, took the road up Coffin Creek.

# Chapter Three

**LEW** Hogan's cabin was built on a bench above Coffin Creek. It was a noisy stream except for a brief period of winter silence, and Nan, who insisted on keeping the windows open in the leanto bedroom, loved the brawling racket of the creek as it poured down from the steep hills. It lulled her to sleep at night; it was the first sound she heard when she woke in the morning.

The sun was slow to reach the cabin because there was a high ridge to the east, so it was not the sunlight that woke her on the morning of the fifteenth. And it was not Ed Lake's hanging. As far as Nan was concerned, the sooner he got his neck stretched the better.

Lew had brought Lake in for dinner one day not long after the fellow had come to Grant County. It was before the first killing, and at the time Nan had no idea what he was or why he was here. But she instinctively disliked him because she sensed a lecherous quality about him that frightened her.

She had not been a virtuous woman. She was not particularly ashamed of her past relationship with George Ballard. She had honestly thought he was going to marry her, and when he had broken off their engagement, she had salvaged her pride by turning to Lew Hogan.

To most women Lew was not a choice catch. He wasn't handsome in the way George Ballard was, and he certainly had little to offer in the way of money or comforts. With him living was often a question of sheer survival.

On the other hand, Lew had many good qualities. He seldom drank or gambled. He was the hardest working man Nan had ever known. He was fanatically loyal to his friends, and that, in Lew's mind, included George Ballard, although Nan knew Ballard was not, and never had been, Lew's friend.

But the main thing was that Lew loved her and he treated her with a deference that pleased and exalted her. In time she had learned to love him, and when life grew monotonous for her and she had the fleeting wish she was living in Gunlock again, she always thought how much better off she was married to Lew than she would have been in Ballard's big house, living with his selfishness and exaggerated ego.

So she had succeeded in putting her past behind her. Lew had taken her as she was, without question, and she enjoyed loving and being loved. Whatever the future brought, she knew she would never be unfaithful to Lew. That was why she had been afraid of Ed Lake. He had only one thing in mind when he was around a woman. She saw it in his big, muscle-ridged face, in his heavy lips and hungry eyes.

When Lew had brought him to the cabin, she

40

had treated him with cool courtesy. Later, when he rode up in the middle of a morning, knowing that Lew was out on the range, she met him with a cocked Winchester and told him never to come here again unless Lew was with him. He never had.

Privately Nan hoped Bill Worden hanged Ed Lake good and high. Everybody would be better off. But Lew did not feel that way. Ever since the trial, he had been worried. They couldn't, he told Nan, let Lake hang, and when she asked him who the "they" was, he became evasive.

But she guessed. Ballard and Jess Ryman and the rest of the ranchers who made up the Grant County Cattlemen's Association. She worried a great deal about it because she knew Lew took anything like this personally, and he was dead set on getting into trouble over it.

Now, looking at him in the thin light that trickled in through the windows, she knew at once he was not asleep and she had a disturbing feeling that he had not slept at all. He opened his eyes and looked at her, but he made no response. She lay motionless for a time, cradling his head in her arms.

"It's tomorrow morning, Nan," he said dully. "We've got to do something and I don't know what to do."

"Lew, Lew," she breathed. "There's nothing we can do. Lake isn't worth your worrying about."

"You don't understand," he said. "I don't like

murder no better than you do, but if Lake hadn't done what he had, we'd have them damned grangers swarming over the creek like grasshoppers."

"They wouldn't bother us," she said. "Not up here where we are. They might settle on George's range, or Jess Ryman's, but this isn't farm land."

He pushed her away. "Nan, you don't savvy this. We're together, George and Jess and all of us. We had to make a stand somewhere and we decided the creek was the line. Once we let one of them sodbusters settle down on this side, we're licked. It's the first one we've got to stop, and that's what Ed done. He did it for us. That's why we can't let 'em hang him."

"Ed Lake never did anything for anybody unless it paid him." She threw back the covers and sat up. "Lew, I love you. You don't know how much I love you, and you don't know what it would do to me if I lost you, or if you got into trouble."

He grinned at her, and sitting up, put an arm around her. He said, "I don't know how I ever got along without you."

"Then be satisfied with just me and what you call a ten-cow spread. You don't have to eat your heart out over a man like Ed Lake."

His arm fell away. "I can't help it, Nan. I've got to do what I can."

"But the law is the law, Lew," she cried. "We can't change it. We can't change Bill Worden, either. If you try to do anything, you'll just get into trouble." She put an arm around his shoulder and scraped her finger tips along his bristly cheek. "Lew, all the land on this side of the creek isn't worth the lives of the three men who were killed."

"I know that now," he said, "but it don't change nothing."

She rose, and putting on her faded robe, went out into the main cabin and built a fire. She set the coffee pot on the front of the stove and returned to the leanto. Lew was still sitting there on the edge of the bed, staring blankly at the wall.

Nan dressed. Then she said, "I'll have breakfast ready by the time you get your clothes on." She went back into the big room and made mush and set the table. She considered telling Lew about Lake's visit that morning and how she had run him off with a Winchester, but he'd think she was making it up to keep him out of trouble.

He came out of the leanto, buttoning his pants and pulling his belt tight. He sat down and ate, to please her, she thought, for it was plain he wasn't hungry. He was barely thirty-one with a receding hair line and a patch of gray at both temples and deep lines under his gray eyes. These last weeks had been ten years to him, and she wanted to cry out in protest against the injustice of it.

She rose, and bringing the coffee pot to the table, said, "I don't understand a man like Ed

43

Lake, but the main thing that gets me is why Jeannie Mason fell in love with him."

When she returned to the table, he asked, "Does anyone understand why you fall in love?" He gave her the slow smile that she liked. "I was in love with you when you had the café and you were engaged to George. I figgered I didn't have no chance, but I was in love with you anyhow."

She lowered her head, wanting to cry and knowing she couldn't, not on this morning of all mornings. She remembered how he used to hang around the café and drink innumerable cups of coffee. George joshed her about it, and at the time she had pitied Lew, never dreaming that someday she would marry him.

"I know," she said finally, and then raised her head to look at him. "But it's different with Jeannie. She never paid any attention to men as long as her mother was alive. I knew her pretty well when I lived in town. She was always, well, kind of mousey."

"Maybe nobody ever paid any attention to her when her mother was alive," Lew said.

Nan nodded. "I suppose that's it. But she's good, Lew. She deserves a better man than Ed Lake."

She wanted to add that Lake never intended marrying Jeannie, but she was in no position to say it. George Ballard never intended marrying her, either. Nan was twenty-eight, coarse-featured and a little too plump, with none of the grace and beauty that was a natural part of Ellen.

44

She'd had her foolish dreams just as Jeannie had had hers, foolish because both of them had trusted the wrong man.

Lew rose. "Don't figger on me for dinner," he said. "I've got a lot of riding to do."

She got up and moved around the table. He wheeled away from her, a little red in the face. He was too honest to fool her, and she didn't press him because she would only make him lie, and as far as she knew, he had never lied to her.

She watched him buckle his gunbelt around him and put on his coat and hat. He was going to see Jess Ryman and the others; they'd try to break Lake out of jail, and they'd wind up in a cell with him. If someone got killed — Worden or McNamara — Lew and the others would hang.

"Don't go, Lew," she cried. "If you love me, don't go."

She ran to him and kissed him; she clung to him with a fierce, unyielding strength, and it was with difficulty that he pulled her arms away from him. "It's something I've got to do," he said doggedly. "Don't make it any harder for me."

He grabbed up his Winchester from where it leaned against the wall and ran out of the house. She stood in the doorway watching him rope and saddle his bay gelding, and when he rode away, she waved to him. He waved back, and kept on down the creek, and presently he disappeared around a bend in the canyon.

She washed and dried the dishes. The only

real happiness she had known had been right here in this cabin, and now Lew was gone and she was haunted by the fear that he would never come back.

Life had been a battle for her from the time she was fourteen. She had made her living since then, sometimes in ways she wanted to forget. She had had not quite two years with Lew, two years when she wanted so many.

She took off her dress and slipped on a pair of Lew's pants, a blue shirt, and her gum boots, and went outside to the garden. Irrigation was work she hated, but it wouldn't be done if she didn't do it. Potatoes, turnips, cabbage, carrots: these were vegetables she could raise and store in the cave Lew had dug in the side of the hill.

Without them their living through the winter would be strictly a meat-and-bread diet. Lew raised a few hogs, and now and then he would bring in a deer. That was his contribution to their living; this was hers.

She was sweaty and dirty and tired when she heard the buggy. Looking up, she saw that it was George Ballard. She leaned on her shovel, mentally condemning him to eternal damnation.

The sun was well up into the sky now, bearing down with its heat here in the narrow canyon, and with typical feminine resentment, she thought he could not have found a worse time to call. Call? No, that wasn't the word. He hadn't made the trip out here to pass the time of day.

Ballard drew up at the edge of the garden and

tipped his hat to her, saying, "Good morning, Nan."

He was driving a span of matched bays, the same team she had ridden behind many times. The only difference was the buggy. This was a new one with red wheels and a mirror on the dashboard. He had bought it for Ellen Worden, she thought, and the old hurt flooded through her for a moment and was gone.

She said harshly, "Lew isn't here."

"I came to see you." He wrapped the lines around the whipstock and stepped down. "It's hot out here. Won't you invite me inside?"

She wiped a hand across her sweaty face; she brushed back a contrary lock of hair, resentment growing. She said, "If you came out here to lord it over me because you found me working like a man . . ."

"Nan, Nan," he broke in. "You know I wouldn't do that. I realize I should have called some Sunday afternoon a long time ago, but I thought it would be better if I didn't."

"It was," she said. "I don't know what brought you here, but I'll guess that it's wrong whatever it is. Go away."

He shook his head, his face grave. "I came here to do you and Lew a favor." He hesitated, then added, "I'm going inside. Please come in. I don't want to talk out here."

He walked around the garden and went on across the hardpacked earth of the yard. He was a fine figure of a man, the kind who usually got what he wanted from a woman. She wondered dully about Ellen Worden. Probably not, Nan thought, not from the daughter of Bill Worden. If Worden suspected anything had gone on between George and Ellen before they were married, he'd use a gun on George and George knew it.

Nan slammed down her shovel and walked to the house. She tugged off her muddy boots and went in. George was sitting in the rocking chair, the one comfortable chair in the house. That was like him, Nan thought, always the best for George Ballard.

"I'll change my clothes." Nan started toward the bedroom, then swung around and came back. "I don't know why I should, for you."

He smiled and nodded. "That's right. I won't stay long."

His hands betrayed his nervousness. They kept dropping into his coat pockets and coming out again, and Nan, watching him, suddenly felt at ease. He wouldn't be here unless he was in trouble, and the idea that George was in trouble filled her with sudden elation.

"George," Nan said, "the best thing you ever did for me was to kick me on my seat and tell me you were tired of me. I was luckier than I deserved, marrying Lew." She sat down on a rawhide-bottom chair and leaned forward. "I love Lew and I'm happy."

"I'm glad, Nan."

He was smooth. He always had been. He

could lie to you by the hour and make you believe every word of it. He probably meant it when he said he was glad. But not for her. Just for himself because she wouldn't be hounding him for something she wanted. She could have given him trouble if she had been of a mind to.

"So you're glad," she murmured. "That's interesting, coming from you."

His big hands were on his thighs, spread wide, and when he spoke, his nervousness appeared in his voice. "Nan, I came here to talk about Lew, not about us. You know Ed Lake is to be hanged in the morning. So far he has not implicated anyone else, but if we don't do something for him, he'll talk and Lew will be in trouble."

She knew George too well to be fooled by that. "You're barking up the wrong tree, George. I can read you like a book." She paused, and then added maliciously, "It might interest you to know that Lew is a better man than you ever were."

She was being mean and she knew it. George took pride in his superiority over other men, and he had little respect for Lew. In spite of himself, he winced, but he recovered his composure at once.

"I am not in a position to argue about a thing like that," he said. "I came to you because someone must do a job before tomorrow morning and Lew is the best one to do it."

"What's the matter with you?"

He drew a cigar from his coat pocket and

busied himself with it for a moment. When he had it going, he said, "You have developed a sharp tongue since you married Lew. You will sharpen your tongue on what I'm going to say now, but I have to say it, for my sake as well as yours and Lew's. This job is one Lew can do, but I can't because of the position I hold in the community."

"You were always one to worry about your reputation," she said.

"Lake expects to be broken out of jail. What he did was in the interest of all of us. Worden has tried to make him name the man who paid him. If he names Lew, you'll be a widow. Worden will hang Lew just as sure as he's going to hang Lake if something isn't done."

Her heart began to pound. She had suspected, as everyone in the county suspected, that some or all of the ranchers had brought Lake to the county and paid him to commit the murders that he had. She didn't think it was Lew, but it could have been if the rest of them had put up the money.

"You want Lew to get Lake out of jail?" she asked finally. "Is that it?"

"Frankly, yes, but at no risk to him. I have a plan, but it calls for help from Jeannie Mason and I can't very well go to her. Lew can. Will you ask Lew to do it?"

She shook her head. "Lew's already determined to get into trouble. I don't aim to give him a push."

"What I propose is the safe way," he said. "Lew's too hotheaded. So is Jess Ryman. If they attack the jail, they're finished. I want to arrange it so Lake will take the risks." He drew a handful of gold coins from his pocket and laid them on the table. "I feel that it is only proper to pay Lew for doing something I can't do. Here is a hundred dollars. Not that it is my responsibility, you understand, but if there is any overt trouble, it will touch all of us who have holdings north of the creek."

She knew, then. It wasn't Lew who had brought Lake to Grant County. It was George. But she had no proof, and whether it was Lew or George, Lew was headed for trouble. George had a good plan or he wouldn't be here, and if it was good enough, it might keep Lew from getting his neck stretched. Besides, there was the money. She needed a new stove. She hadn't bought a new dress for a year. Or a hat.

"What is your plan?" she asked.

George showed his relief. "That's better, Nan. You're the smartest woman I know, and I might say married life has agreed with you."

"I've gained twenty pounds," she said tartly. "Now about your plan."

He laid a short-barreled gun on the table beside the money. "All that Lake needs is a gun. I want Lew to go to Jeannie and have her bake Lake a pie. Or a cake if that would be better. They'll give him anything he wants that's within reason. Have her put about thirty feet of twine

51

inside the cake. Tonight, say around ten o'clock, tell him to let the twine out of the cell window and have Lew tie the gun to it. After Lake gets the gun it's up to him."

She thought about it and she could see little risk to it. Jeannie would do her part. And there was practically no danger to Lew if all he had to do was to tie the gun to the string. If Lake got shot while he was trying to make a jail break, that was exactly what he deserved.

"All right," she said. "I'll tell Lew."

George rose. He looked down at her for a moment, frowning. Then he said, "I never knew you to break your word, and I'm sure Lew will do his part."

, She remained in her chair while George walked to the door. He turned, his hat in his hand, still frowning. "If you have a notion that I'm giving you a weapon to use against me, remember one thing. I will deny any part in this business. You know I'll be believed, not you, so don't try it."

"Yes," she murmured. "I would expect you to deny it."

He wheeled and strode out. She remained sitting there until she heard his buggy leave the yard. Then, quite suddenly it occurred to her that there was no reason she couldn't do this herself and leave Lew completely out of it.

She went into the leanto and changed to a blouse and riding skirt. She hid the money in an empty can on a shelf behind the stove, put the revolver into her pocket, and left the house. She saddled her bay mare and started for town.

The more she thought about this, the better she liked it. Before Lew and Ryman and the others got around to doing anything, Ed Lake would be dead, or on his way to freedom.

# Chapter Four

**WHEN** McNamara returned to the jail with Ed Lake's breakfast, Bill Worden sent him to the hotel to order a chicken supper for Lake. He was scowling when he returned, for he had been thinking about it, and it struck him all wrong.

"Must be a tough old rooster," he said sourly, "having to order it at eight o'clock in the morning."

"I was afraid I'd forget it," Worden said.

McNamara rolled a cigarette, his anger bringing a white line around his mouth. "Bill, why in hell do we have to pamper a back-shooting killer like Ed Lake? That Smith boy he killed didn't have no chicken for supper, I'll bet. And his brothers and dad ain't having chicken for supper tonight, either."

"Probably not." Worden rose wearily from where he had been sitting at the desk. "Just a custom, Mac. I asked Lake what he wanted and he said chicken and dumplings."

McNamara lit his cigarette and put the match out with a savage jerk. "Why can't we take him out and hang him now? I don't like it, Bill. The town's too quiet."

Gunlock was always quiet at eight o'clock in the morning; it meant nothing today. But there

54

was as much tension in Bill Worden as there was in McNamara. Mac was thinking, Bill told himself, that a lot could happen in twenty-four hours. And that was exactly what Worden was thinking.

"According to Judge Webb, we're ordered to hang Lake at nine o'clock on the morning of June sixteenth," Worden said. "That's official, so it's the law. You and me don't ask questions, Mac. We just do what we're told."

McNamara snorted. "You ought to write a book, Bill. If you had nine hundred pages, that's all you'd say."

"I guess it's all there is to say," Worden said.

He wasn't hungry, but he knew he'd have a headache before noon if he didn't eat. Leaving the courthouse, he crossed the lawn to the Chinaman's and ordered a stack of flapjacks. He drank two cups of coffee, thinking how many times in eleven years the same questions had occurred to him.

The law was not a flexible thing. From Worden's point of view, Ed Lake should have been hanged weeks ago, but it had been Judge Webb's business to set the date, not Worden's. As far as Lake's meal of chicken and dumplings was concerned, it was a matter of custom. Worden would have been criticized if he hadn't asked him what he wanted for his last meal. Not that Worden was afraid of criticism. It was simply common sense to avoid as much as he could.

When he left the restaurant, he remembered a chore he had been putting off and knew he could postpone it no longer. As he glanced along Main Street, the sun, hard and bright on its white dust, it struck him that McNamara was right. The town was too quiet. There wasn't a horse or rig racked anywhere along the street. No one was in sight. Just a cur dog that belonged to the Barton boy. He was dozing in the sun, a brown spot in the dust.

Worden turned down a side street to the white cottage where the preacher, John Harris, lived. Even in matters of religion, Gunlock was divided. There was Preacher Rigdon's church that was attended by the farmers, a new church that had been built since Worden had become sheriff. And there was Harris' Community Church that was attended by the townspeople and ranchers, mostly by the women. It was there when Worden had come to the county.

Worden did not belong to either, but Ada and Ellen attended Harris' church. Now Worden was a little hesitant about going to Harris. He might be asked where he was every Sunday morning, and that would be a hard question to answer to a preacher.

But he misjudged Harris, who opened the door to his knock and invited him in. Harris was an old man, slight of build, with white hair and a flowing white mustache, gentle and soft-spoken, a striking contrast to Rigdon who was a violent man.

Worden shook his head at Harris' invitation to sit down. "Can't stay, Parson. I've got a favor to ask. I don't think Ed Lake will want to see a preacher, but it's customary for a condemned man to have a chance at one. And it's customary for a preacher to be on hand when the execution takes place. I was wondering if you'd do it."

Harris nodded. "Of course, Mr. Worden. As a matter of fact, I've been to see him on two different occasions. McNamara was on duty both times. He may not have mentioned it to you."

"No, he probably forgot it."

Harris smiled ruefully. "All I got for my trouble was a cursing, but I'll be glad to try again. Sometimes a man's feelings about God change when the time is short. The trouble before was Lake seemed to be sure he wouldn't hang."

"He still thinks he won't."

"Mr. Worden," Harris said, "I offer this suggestion hesitantly because you are a brave and capable man. So is McNamara. But there are only two of you. I understand that some of Lake's friends intend to break him out of jail, and there is also talk that the farmers plan to lynch him because they're afraid he'll get away."

"That kind of puts my tail in a crack, doesn't it, Parson?"

"In a manner of speaking, that's exactly what it does. I'm afraid you're so close to this thing that you don't realize it's become a famous case. The Denver newspapers have been full of it."

"I haven't looked at a paper lately," Worden said.

He hadn't because he had not wanted to know what the reporters were writing. Several had been in town. They would certainly be on hand in the morning. To Worden they were as annoying as a flock of gnats in a man's ear, and just about as useful.

"My suggestion is simply this," Harris hurried on. "I know the governor personally. If you'll permit me, I'll wire him that the situation is serious and we need a company of the National Guard to keep order." He sensed he had made a mistake, and added hastily, "Or perhaps it would be better if you wired the governor."

Worden bit his lower lip. The things he felt like saying would be wrong. Harris was only doing what he thought was right. Worden said mildly, "You know the story about the riot in Texas. Somebody hollered for help, and one ranger showed up. When they asked him why a whole bunch of rangers weren't sent, he said, 'Only one riot, isn't there?' Well, we've got one man to hang and we've got one sheriff."

Worden put his hat on his head and left the house. He should be insulted, he thought, but it was the sort of thing he could expect. Before the day was over, he'd have more of the same.

He thought about it as he walked back to the courthouse. After eleven years on a job like this, a man gets so he thinks he can handle anything. Worden had never had more than one deputy, and McNamara was the best. If he needed another man, he could call on the courthouse janitor, Orval Jones, who often doubled as jailer when Worden and McNamara were out on a case.

As he walked slowly through the hot sunshine, the thought occurred to him that perhaps he was being too sure of himself, too proud. In a case that had the publicity this one had, he'd have real trouble if Lake broke jail.

It would make the whole county look bad, and the farmers would have more fuel for their gossip. Collusion, they'd say. The sheriff had his reasons for not sending for help. George Ballard was a stockman, and Ballard was going to be Worden's son-in-law, wasn't he? It was as plain as the nose on your face.

The reporters would make something out of that. Worden's name would be in the headlines from coast to coast. But by the time he reached his office, he had made up his mind. To send for help at this hour would be an admission of abject weakness, and by God, he wasn't weak.

He had some paper work to do, but he found it impossible to keep his mind on it. He kept getting up from his desk and looking out of the window at the gallows. He yanked his watch out of his vest pocket every five minutes and looked at it, but the hand seemed to be stuck. Finally, he went down to the basement to get Orval Jones.

Jones had been janitor as long as Worden had

59

been sheriff. He was a little man with false teeth that clacked irritatingly when he talked, and he had illusions about his potential ability as a lawman. He read every dime novel he could get his hands on, and whenever he had the slightest opportunity, he assured Worden he would be a first-class deputy if Mac ever quit. He was still hurt because he had been overlooked when Mac was hired.

"Come up and keep an eye on Lake for awhile," Worden said. "Mac and me have to check the gallows."

"Glad to, sheriff, glad to." Jones dived into the cubbyhole where he slept and cooked his meals. He came out with an ancient Navy Colt stuck in his waistband, a needle gun in one hand, and a double-barreled shotgun in the other. "You can count on me, Sheriff."

Worden climbed the two flights of stairs with Jones, saying nothing because he didn't want to give the janitor any encouragement to talk. This morning the clacking of the man's teeth jarred on his nerves more than ever.

When they reached the jail, Worden said, "Orval's going to spell you off, Mac. We'll take a look at the gallows before it gets any hotter."

"Go right ahead, Mac." Jones laid the shotgun and needle gun across the desk and drew the Colt from his waistband. "If anybody tries to take that heller out of custody, I'll blow his head off so fast it'll get to hell before his soul does."

McNamara beat Worden through the door. As

they walked along the hall, he grumbled, "I dunno which is worse, to hear Orval talk with his teeth in his mouth and flopping around like an old mare's tail in the wind, or hear him without his teeth and have him whistling on every word."

Worden grinned. "Hard question to decide." When they reached the first floor, he asked, "How heavy do you reckon Lake is?"

" 'Bout two hundred, I'd say," McNamara answered.

"That's what I figured," Worden said.

There was no wind, and not even a trace of a cloud in the brassy sky. The heat made a man sweat in every pore of his body. Worden seldom felt the heat, and now he wondered if it was really hot, or if it was just the way he felt today. When they passed Al Good's hardware store, Worden glanced at the thermometer. The mercury stood squarely at the hundred-mark.

"Hell for June," McNamara said.

Worden nodded. "Going to be hard on the grass if we don't get some rain." Then he wondered why he was worrying about the grass. If there wasn't any grass in Grant County, there wouldn't be any stockmen, and if there were no stockmen, he'd have no trouble hanging Ed Lake.

They borrowed two sacks from the feed store, took them down to the creek and filled them with sand, then carried them to the store and weighed them. Too heavy, so they emptied out some of the sand and weighed them again. This time Worden had the weight he wanted.

Luke Prentice who owned the feed store watched with close interest. He asked finally, "Reckon that booger's gonna hang in the morning?"

Worden straightened and glared at Prentice. This question had been asked too many times. He shouted, "You're damned right he'll hang."

Frightened, Prentice backed away. "You don't need to get your dander up, Sheriff, but there's a lot of talk floating around. Lew Hogan was in town the other day getting a sack of corn for his hogs, and he says, 'Luke, I know Ed Lake pretty well and I don't figure he shot that . . .' " He stopped. Worden and McNamara had picked up the sacks of sand and were walking out.

When they reached the street, McNamara said, "Bill, if we need any help, and I'm not saying we will, mind you, but if we do, we'll have to get it from rabbits like Luke Prentice."

"Yeah," Worden muttered. "From rabbits."

Funny how certain thoughts kept running through a man's mind until they cut a channel there, like heavy rains that continually deepened the gullies on a hillside. What Mac had just said had occurred to Worden countless times since he had been sheriff.

Now, more than ever, he wondered why he had run for sheriff in the first place. You risk your life for men like Luke Prentice. They cheer you on, or give you hell if you make a mistake, and not one in a hundred ever says "thank you" or whatever. Crazy thinking, he told himself. A man didn't pin a star on his shirt for the thanks he'd get. Anyhow, you couldn't use thanks to buy groceries from Tad Barton.

It took only a few moments to climb to the gallows, lay the sacks of sand on the trap, and spring it. The sacks spilled to the ground below, and McNamara grunted, "Sure wish that was Lake."

"Empty the sand out and take the sacks back to Prentice," Worden said. Then he added, "With thanks."

McNamara gave him a tight grin. "Sure. With thanks."

Back in his office Worden tried to write a letter answering a Utah sheriff who wanted to know if a man named Slim Brace, alias Wagon Tongue Sawhill, had been seen in Grant County. It was a simple task that would ordinarily have been completed in five minutes, but it was after twelve when he finished.

He glanced into the jail before he left, saw that McNamara was back, and left the courthouse. He thought of getting his dinner downtown and decided against it. Ada didn't know he wasn't coming home and it always bothered her if she got his dinner and he didn't show up.

But when he reached his house and went in, he saw that Ada and Ellen had turned the living room into a dressmaker's parlor with white cloth, lace, pins, needles, pieces of pattern, thimbles, and scissors scattered all over the room. The kitchen table wasn't even set.

"You going to cook dinner or not?" Worden shouted. "I can't stay here all day. Want me to go to the hotel?"

Ada dropped her needle and rose, a lapful of cloth falling to the floor. He hadn't shouted at her that way for years, and he saw she was hurt. She said, "It'll just take a minute, Bill. I guess the time got away from me."

How could it, he wondered. This had been the slowest morning since the creation. He was still irritated, and he asked sharply, "Ada, why don't you get Jeannie Mason to make Ellen's wedding dress?"

Horrified, Ellen whispered, "Daddy, you know I couldn't."

Ada walked out of the room, her back very straight. Worden found a place on the couch to sit down. He filled his pipe and lighted it, impatient at the delay. Leaning back, he stretched his long legs in front of him, his eyes on Ellen.

She was standing in the middle of the room, studying the pattern intently. She was too young to get married, he thought, too young for a man like George Ballard who was twelve years older than she was, too young even if Ballard was the man she thought he was.

If the farmers were right about Ballard . . . But there he went again. He had no proof. After the hanging he'd know. If Ballard did not make a move to save Lake, he could be sure there was no basis for the gossip about the man.

64

"Ellen." Her attention was riveted so closely upon the pattern that she did not hear him, so he said, "Ellen," again, louder this time.

She looked up. "I'm sorry. What is it?"

He took the pipe out of his mouth, wishing now he hadn't said anything. "I hate to lose you."

She laughed and wrinkled her nose at him. "You won't lose me. You know what they say when your daughter gets married. You gain a son."

"I suppose so," he said, and getting up, went into the kitchen.

Ada had his meal on the table before he thought she could, mostly leftovers from the night before that she had warmed up. But he didn't say anything. She had set just one plate. When he asked, "Aren't you and Ellen eating today?" she said, "After a while. We can't quit just now."

But she sat down at her usual place. He said, "Go on back to work. I don't need any help to eat."

She shook her head. "Bill, you're in a temper today. I'll bet you didn't have any breakfast. Why didn't you wake me this morning?"

"I couldn't," he said. "You were sleeping like a baby."

She was silent. He went on eating, forcing the food down because he had to, now that she had fixed it. He glanced at her, noticing the slight frown on her forehead. Something was bothering her, and he wondered if she had heard the talk about Ed Lake. It would be a miracle if she hadn't, but there were times when she seemed to live on an island in the midst of reality.

Presently Ada said, "You shouldn't have said anything about Jeannie Mason, Bill. Ellen knows what she is."

"That hasn't got a damned thing to do with her dressmaking," he said hotly. "I don't know what she lives on. Every other woman in town thinks the same way you do."

"It's her own fault," Ada said stiffly. "If she's going to live . . . immorally, she can expect to be treated the way she has been."

"If a woman makes one mistake . . ."

"She's been making the same mistake ever since Ed Lake came to town," Ada snapped. "She should be run out of Gunlock."

Worden pushed back his chair and got up. That was the way it went, he thought. Let a woman trip and fall on her face, and every other woman saw to it she stayed on her face. He said, "I won't be home tonight. I've got to stay in the courthouse."

She rose and came around the table to him. "You'll be all right, won't you, Bill?"

He knew, then, that she had heard. When he said, "Sure, I'll be all right," the frown left her forehead. She kissed him, and he put his arms around her and held her hard. After all these years of married life, he still liked to kiss her, liked to feel her body pressed against his, and when he left the house, he saw that the old familiar serenity was in her face again. It was her vote of confidence that he could handle any situation that faced him; it was exactly what he needed.

# Chapter Five

**WHEN** the door of George Ballard's private office closed, there was nothing for Jeannie Mason to do but walk out of the bank. She stumbled into the blinding sunshine and went on across the street, almost stepping on the Barton boy's dog that was dozing in the dust. He opened his eyes, looked at her reproachfully, and went on sleeping.

Jeannie made the turn at the corner and climbed the hill toward her house. She had the feeling she was sleepwalking, that this was a horrible dream, and while she was dreaming, two high walls were closing in on her, squeezing time into eternity until now there were less than twenty-four hours left.

She stopped, feeling the morning's dry heat press against her head and neck and back. No, this was not a dream. She put a hand to her throat, her eyes on George Ballard's big house, and she thought how it would be to have a rope around her neck and then be dropped and have the noose snap up hard under her chin.

She shivered and went on, walking slowly, remembering how it had always been with the Ballards, the first family to come to the valley, the first to build a fine town house, the first to start a bank. Before Bill Worden's day, Long-horn Ballard with the bristling mustache and piercing brown eyes had dictated to the Grand County sheriffs.

Old Longhorn, picturesque and stubborn and overbearing, had made the Ballard name mean what it did. If he were alive today, he'd have had Ed Lake out of jail before now, law or no law, tough sheriff or an easy one. Alec, George's father, had been about half the man Longhorn was, and George was less man than Alec had been. At least that was what Jeannie's mother had often said, and she'd known all three.

"The Ballard blood is running pretty thin," Mrs. Mason used to say with considerable satis-faction. "George don't do things for himself the way his grandfather did. Smart, George is, but in a country like this, he'll find out he can't get everything he wants by shoving folks around like checkers."

Jeannie reached her house at the end of the street, opened the gate in the picket fence, and walked up the path. She went inside and stood there for a moment, leaving the door open. This room had not changed as long as she could remember. The horsehair sofa, the stuffed owl on the mantel, the framed forget-me-nots on the wall with the embroidered words, "Home, Sweet Home": all exactly as they had been when her mother had died.

Jeannie sat down in the scarred rocking chair,

and leaning her head against the antimacassar that covered the back, gripped the arms until her knuckles were white. Her mother had been a strong-willed person who had sensed a certain kinship of spirit with old Longhorn Ballard. Jeannie could not remember her father, but he must have been a weak man. Jeannie often suspected that her mother had overpowered him so completely that death had been a sanctuary for him.

Mrs. Mason had not needed a man. She had been an expert dressmaker and milliner, and she had seen to it that Jeannie was as skilled as she was. They had made a good living here in Gunlock, if clothes to wear and food to eat and a place to sleep were the elements that made a good living. But Jeannie had been smothered by her mother until she had not even considered having a thought of her own until she asked permission.

Jeannie had grown up without having a beau. She had never gone to a dance, and if she went to a picnic or a basket social, her mother was always on hand like a big-bosomed setting hen, clucking in a manner that ran the boys off as effectively as if she had pinned a sign on Jeannie that read "poison."

But Jeannie had had her dreams of romance, and as she watched other girls her age going to dances or taking buggy rides with boys, she learned to hate her mother with the fierce abandon of youth. Her mother had never known. The whole trouble was that Mrs. Mason had no one to love but Jeannie, so her love had become a cruel, possessive force.

Now that her mother had been dead for a year and a half, Jeannie had almost forgotten how much she had hated her. Ed Lake had come along and Jeannie had begun to live. All the things she had missed as a girl were hers now. They were still hers, even with Ed in jail, at least in the spirit.

She began to rock, unaware of the heat, forgetting she had had no breakfast and it would soon be time for dinner. She remembered how it had started, that first day Ed had ridden into town on his black gelding, a big and handsome man who had never known her mother.

Jeannie was in Barton's store buying some dress goods when she saw Ed ride in. She watched him dismount and talk briefly to Bill Worden and Mike McNamara, then go into the hotel. She lingered over her choice of cloth until Ted Barton had become irritated with her. She kept wondering if the stranger would have his dinner and ride on as so many others did. Or if he stayed, would she ever meet him?

She finally left the store, her arms full of bundles. There was a mean wind that day that drove a white cloud of dust the length of the street. Half blinded and walking with her head down, she bumped into Ed and her packages had fallen all over the sidewalk. That's the way it had started, an accident which would have stopped there if her mother had been alive.

She had loved Ed's big laugh and his friendly face. They stooped to pick up her bundles and cracked heads and Ed laughed again. He said, "Well, the least I can do is to carry your things home for you." He did, and she asked him in for a glass of lemonade. He might stay around, he told her. Maybe buy a ranch, he added, his bold black eyes on her.

When he left, she'd thought she would never see him again. She had no illusions about her beauty and figure. Other men who had known her all her life considered her an old maid at twenty-four, and the ones who were looking for wives passed her up for younger girls. Even now she did not know what had brought him back that evening, but he'd come and asked her to take a walk with him. After that she'd seen him almost every day until he'd been arrested for the Smith boy's murder.

Ed had never been one to talk about his past. She knew he played cards and won, and that he rode a great deal, saying he was looking for a ranch. She didn't ask questions, content to accept him at face value, loving him as she had never loved anyone in her life. Then, and the truth came to her with brutal force, she realized that she wasn't getting any work, that no one was even calling on her. She had become, in the words she had heard from her mother so often, "a bad woman."

She didn't care, not as long as she had Ed. He

talked rather vaguely about marrying her, but never permitted her to pin him down to a date. There were nights when she didn't sleep, wondering if he would just ride off as he had come, leaving her and forgetting her, but she always found assurance in the thought that he loved her as much as she loved him.

She kept drawing on her savings, spending grudgingly, and then only for food. Ed ate most of his meals with her, and occasionally gave her a few dollars, handing them to her with a flourish as if he were being very generous. That was a side of him she did not understand, but she mentally excused him on the grounds that he was saving his money to buy a ranch.

After he was arrested, her sympathy was all for Ed, and she blamed the murdered Smith boy for what had happened. If Ed had killed him, and she was finally forced to accept the truth, the Smith boy must have done something to make Ed do it. But he refused to give any explanation.

The day after he was arrested, Jeannie went to see him, and he told her to ask at the post office for his mail. He said to open a letter if one was there, and if she found money, to send for a Denver lawyer that Ed knew.

The letter was there, Ed's name and address printed neatly in pencil. Inside was a thousand dollars, and a note promising he wouldn't hang if he did not incriminate anyone else. She sent for the lawyer. He came, did nothing for Ed at the trial, and took most of the money. Since then she had been living on what was left of the thousand dollars.

Once when she was visiting Ed in jail, she asked, "If you shot Smith, why don't you plead guilty and tell why you did it?"

But he only laughed at her. "Don't you worry, honey. George Ballard will see they don't put a rope on my neck."

"Ballard never did anything for anybody," she cried. "Why do you think he will for you?"

Ed laughed again. "He's got to. You'll see."

That's the way it had been every day, even after he was sentenced. Last night for the first time Ed showed a little concern. He said, "I don't know what Ballard's got up his sleeve, but he'd better have something pretty damned good. Come morning you go see him and tell him he'll be mighty sorry if he don't get me out of here."

So she had gone to Ballard and he had said exactly what she had been sure he would. She had no friends now, so she had no way of knowing what was being said in town. But she knew Gunlock. There was gossip, plenty of it, and perhaps some of it concerned Ed and George Ballard.

Now, because there was so little time left, she tried to think of something she could do. She had wondered about the money, but Ed refused to tell her anything about it. Only one thing made sense, and she finally reached the point where she admitted it to herself. Someone had paid Ed for the Smith boy's murder.

She recoiled from the thought. To her Ed had always been kind and gentle, and it was incredible that he was capable of cold-blooded murder. So she had to fall back on the only thought that would sustain her; he had done it in self-defense. She loved him; therefore she must believe in him, and believing in him forced her to try to think of something she could do for him.

The hours fled by. The day grew hotter. There was no sound but the steady groaning of her chair as she rocked. She had to do something today or tonight. Tomorrow would be too late. But she was helpless against men like Bill Worden and Mike McNamara. Then she heard someone knock and looking up, she saw Nan Hogan standing on the porch.

Jeannie rose, uncertain of herself. She walked to the door, remembering she had not made a dress for Nan since she had married Lew. Jeannie said, "How are you, Nan?"

"I'm hot." Nan took off her hat and wiped her face that was wet with sweat. "May I come in?"

Jeannie hesitated. "It's been a long time since anyone came to see me. I'm . . . well, maybe you don't know . . ."

"I know," Nan said, "but it doesn't make any difference to me. I'm no better than you are, Jeannie, and I've got a hunch that most of the women in this town aren't, either. Not in their thoughts, anyhow."

"I'll be glad to have you come in," Jeannie said, and stepped aside.

Nan moved through the door, blowing out a great breath of air. "Lordy, it's hot. A thunder storm's coming, though. That'll cool things off."

Nan dropped down on the couch and stretched her legs in front of her. She had never been a lady, Jeannie thought, and she didn't want to be. Probably that was why George Ballard hadn't married her. She was wide of hip and often loud of voice, and when she had operated the restaurant, she'd had all the business she wanted. Men liked her, and she hadn't cared what the women thought.

"I'll start a fire and make some tea," Jeannie said.

"No, you won't," Nan said quickly. "It's hot enough in here without a fire." She motioned toward the rocking chair. "Sit down, Jeannie. I came on business and my business isn't dressmaking." She laughed. "Not that I don't need some dresses, but I can't afford to pay you."

Jeannie sat down in the rocking chair, her hands folded primly in front of her. She must be a queer one to a woman like Nan, she thought. She probably looked and acted like an old maid, but she wasn't, she thought with fierce pride. She was Ed Lake's woman. Nan knew it and she didn't care.

Her obligation as a hostess worried her. She said, "I could make some lemonade."

Nan shook her head and wiped her red, sweaty

face with a sleeve. "I just want to talk, Jeannie. I've got a proposition that's important to both of us. You and me are kind of alike. Lew isn't much, not the way most folks think, but I love him. Ed Lake's no good, Jeannie, just no good, but you love him, don't you?"

"He is good," Jeannie cried. "He's always been good to me. If he did kill the Smith boy, he must have had a reason."

"Sure," Nan said. "He was paid to do it. According to George Ballard, Lew was the one who paid him."

Jeannie froze. Her hands tightened on her lap. She was the only one besides Ed who knew about the thousand dollars, except, of course, the one who sent it. But it wasn't Lew. He could barely write his name, and she remembered how the printing on the envelope had looked. Each letter made with neat precision, every word correctly spelled. But she wasn't going to tell Nan that.

"You want to get Ed out of jail, don't you?" Nan asked.

Jeannie nodded, unable to say anything. Nan had been brutally truthful when she'd said Ed had been paid to kill young Smith. All this time Jeannie had ducked the truth because she didn't want to believe it. She didn't now. She cried out, "Of course I want to get Ed out. I won't believe what you said. I won't."

Nan said, a little pityingly, "It's a weakness in us women to try to see something good in our men, and if we can't, we make it up. I was that way with George before I married Lew, but right down inside me I knew he was no good all the time."

Nan smiled and shook her head. "You know, Jeannie, I'm as crazy as you are, but I don't want to lose Lew. If I don't do something, he'll wind up where Ed is. George didn't say this, but I got the notion that the cattlemen's association paid Ed to shoot the Smith boy. Of course he doesn't want Ed saying that out loud, so he suggested we get him out of jail. I'm willing to break the law to do it."

"But how . . ."

"We'll do the job, you and me. If they don't hang Ed, he won't talk, and Lew won't be in trouble. As far as I'm concerned, it's that simple. Now then. It's going to be dark tonight. No moon, and if that thunder storm develops, the sky will be cloudy. There's just one thing. Will Worden let you take a pie or cake to Ed?"

"Yes," Jeannie said eagerly. "I'm sure he will. He has several times."

"Then it won't be hard." Nan drew a gun from her pocket and laid it on the couch beside her. "George gave this to me, but you can't smuggle it into the jail. Worden might catch on, so we'll bake a pie and put some strong twine inside. You tell Ed to let the string out of the window at ten o'clock tonight. I'll tie the gun to it. All he's got to do is to pull it up. After that it'll be up to him."

Jeannie rose, wondering why she hadn't

78

thought of it. "I'll go down to the courthouse now and ask Worden if I can bake a pie for his supper."

Nan laughed shakily. "I was afraid you wouldn't do it. We're a couple of fools, you know, risking a prison sentence for a couple of men who aren't worth it. Well, I'll bake the pie if you've got some twine that will work."

"I have some. I'll start the fire. I'll open up a jar of cherries. Ed likes cherry pie."

"This is one he'll sure like," Nan said.

Five minutes later Jeannie left the house, walking fast, wanting to be sure about this. She found Worden alone in his office, sitting at his desk as he stared blankly at the wall in front of him. He rose when Jeannie came in. He said, "I suppose you want to see Lake."

Jeannie leaned against the door jamb, breathing hard from her walk, her heart hammering in her chest. She started to speak, but she shut her mouth without saying anything. She couldn't fail now, but as she looked at the sheriff's strong, craggy face, she wondered if it would work. No one had fooled him since he'd been elected. The best sheriff Grant County ever had, folks said, and it was Ed's bad luck to have him in office at this time.

Worden came to her and taking her arm, led her to a chair. He said, "I know how you feel, Jeannie. He isn't worth it, but telling you that doesn't change anything, does it?"

"No," she whispered, and wondered why so

many people said Worden was a hard, unfeeling man. "I came to ask a favor, Mr. Worden. I want to do something for Ed. He likes cherry pie. Could I bring him one for supper?"

"You sure can," Worden said. "He'll have a good supper. He asked for chicken and dumplings. I'm getting it from the hotel."

Jeannie rose. "Thank you, Mr. Worden. I'll bring the pie about six."

"You want to see him now?"

She shook her head. "I'd like to visit with him when I bring the pie."

"You'll have your visit," Worden said. "If I'm not here, I'll tell Mac."

She fled then, afraid she would give something away. If she stayed, he would see it in her face. When she left the courthouse, she noticed the black mass of clouds that had rolled up around Red Mountain. Already the air was cooler. Nan had been right. If they were lucky, the sky would be overcast tonight.

She must ask Ed where he was going, she thought, and she would meet him there. But both of them would need money. She had nothing except her house. She couldn't sell it in the short time she had, but Ballard might lend a few hundred dollars to her. He had to.

She turned toward the bank. She had never blackmailed anyone in her life, but she was going to now.

# Chapter Six

**FROM** his office window, Bill Worden could see the gallows, and he could look past it to Main Street that was still as empty as it had been that morning, an emptiness that reminded him of the quiet heat of the day. But a storm was coming, the afternoon already beginning to cool. He could not, he thought, stop this storm of nature any more than he could stop the human storm that was coming.

He thought about Jeannie Mason with her ash-blond hair and pale blue eyes and thin body that seemed so completely lacking in animal vitality. She could do wonders with her needle for other women, but her own dresses were always plain, made of somber-hued cloth with none of the bright touches she lavished on the dresses she was hired to make.

Jeannie's mother had been a virago, a heavy, massive-bosomed woman who had moved with the grace and elasticity of a loaded hayrack. She had tried once to organize a woman's club and failed, and she had often written letters which had been published in the Gunlock *Weekly Herald* denouncing men and their ways. Men were necessary to perpetuate the race, she had reluctantly admitted, but aside from that, they were unnecessary and she had committed all of them to perdition.

Worden could understand how Jeannie, held in subjection so long by her mother, had fallen in love with Ed Lake. But why Lake had picked out a shy, skim-milk woman like Jeannie was something Worden did not understand at all. Things like that, Worden knew, were often beyond human understanding. You had to accept them as fact whether they made sense or not.

During the weeks after the trial Worden had sensed the terrible fear that gripped Jeannie, and he sympathized with her because he knew her fear was a genuine and exhausting human emotion. She had lost weight; her eyes were always red from weeping, although she tried to appear bright and encouraging when she came to visit Lake. But she had not given up hope, and he wondered about it, now that time had almost run out. The governor had refused clemency, and the last appeal to a higher court had failed.

Worden was still pondering it when Doc Quinn and Judge Webb came in. They were old men who dated their residence in Grant County far back beyond the time Worden had come to the valley. And, like old men who had lived their lives in such a way as to earn the respect of others, they were a little too sure of their judgment and the validity of their advice.

They had something in their minds, Worden saw, and he felt the quick anger of a man whose nerves were already drawn so tight that it took an effort to appear even decently polite.

"Howdy, Judge," Worden said. "Howdy, Doc. Come in and sit."

They said, "Howdy," and sat down in two of the rawhide-bottom chairs which lined one wall. Quinn took off his derby and ran a hand through his thin white hair, plainly ill at ease. Webb was a few years younger than Quinn, tall and stooped and frail. He had been sick much of the previous winter, and as Worden moved back across the room to his desk and sat down, he told himself that the Judge would not make it through another winter.

"Looks like it's going to blow up a storm," Worden said.

Quinn nodded. "Hope so. Been hotter'n the hinges of hell today. Don't ever remember June being this hot. Do you, Judge?"

"No." Webb took a blackened meerschaum pipe from his pocket and filled the bowl. "Bill, there's no use beating around the bush. The town's too quiet."

Worden nodded. "I know."

"Just one of those crazy things that happens once in awhile to a man who represents the law when you get two factions of society that can't see anything but their own side of it. In a way it illustrates something good in people. With the ranchers it's loyalty to a man they believe is on their side. On the other hand the farmers know that the law is their only protection, and they're afraid the mandate of the court will not be carried out."

Worden picked up his pipe where he had laid it on his desk, his gaze shuttling from Webb to Quinn and back to the Judge. He laid the pipe down. He said truculently, "Judge, if you think I won't get Lake hanged legal and proper, you just forget it."

"You'll hang him if you're permitted to," Webb said, "but I know how things are shaping up. Sometime during the night the ranchers are going to make a try at busting Lake out."

"And what can you and McNamara do except get yourselves shot?" Quinn demanded. "Put that bunch together, the little fry, I mean, along with Jiggs Larribee and the Lazy B crew, and you'll be fighting twenty men."

"Then we'll fight them," Worden said harshly, "and they'll make outlaws out of themselves."

Webb lighted his pipe and pulled on it. He didn't have enough teeth to grip the stem, so he held it with one hand. He sat with his long skinny legs stretched in front of him, his head against the wall, a tired, sick old man.

Worden felt like a callow youngster in the presence of these two, and because of that, his irritation grew. They had made their contribution to the taming of a wild land, and they were not convinced that anyone else could take up where they left off. They were the old ones, the tribal leaders.

"There's something else," Webb went on.

"The farmers are as dangerous as the ranchers. There's twice as many of them, and they're bound to make an issue out of this. You can't blame them. Lake has become a symbol. If he's hanged, it will discourage further violence. If he escapes, then the law has been flouted, and they know the ranchers will wind up running them out of the country."

"Not as long as I'm sheriff," Worden snapped.

Webb jabbed his pipestem at Worden. "That's exactly the point, Bill. You'll be dead, and the cattlemen's association will pick the next man who wears the star. I don't want you dead, Bill."

Worden got up and walked to the window. "You're beating around the bush, Judge. Let's have it."

Webb pulled on his pipe. "Two reporters came in on the afternoon train. There'll be some more before morning. This is big, Bill. It's a test of the whole principle of law. It means something to me, and I think it does to you."

"Doc, if you don't get to the point . . ."

"Here it is," Doc Quinn cut in. "If we wire the governor, we could have a company of the National Guard here before midnight. We've contacted the governor. He has a company of the Guard standing by."

At any other time and under any other circumstances, Worden would have held his temper, but now it was too much. He stalked toward the two old men, his face red. "I ought to kick your butts right out of my office," he shouted. "Did that damned preacher get to you with his fine ideas?"

Quinn and Webb looked blank. Webb asked, "You mean Rigdon?"

"No. Harris."

"Haven't seen him all day," Webb said. "This is our idea. We took it on ourselves . . ."

"You took it on yourselves," Worden mimicked. "Judge, did I ever tell you how to handle a case when you were on the bench? No sir, I never did, and by the same token, I'll run my end of things without your interference."

Webb bent toward the spittoon and knocked his pipe out. He said, "I was afraid you'd take it that way. You're wrong, Bill. You and Mike McNamara add up to a total of two men. I told you the ranchers will have twenty. If the farmers try to do the hanging, you'll be up against forty or fifty. It's too big for you, Bill."

"Judge," Worden said, laboring with his breathing, "it's the same to me if there's ten thousand. I swore I'd uphold the law, and I didn't expect any help from the National Guard when I took the oath. Now if that's all you've got to say . . ."

"Not quite," Doc Quinn said. "You're a good man, Bill. You've got guts and savvy, and you've never failed doing your job, but this is too big and it means too much to take any chances."

Worden stomped back to his desk and sat down. For a long moment he glared at the old men. His hot anger cooled. He was a little

86

ashamed of what he had said and how he had said it. But for all their age, they were wrong. More than any other man, Bill Worden had seen to it that law had become something more than theory, that the decisions Judge Webb handed down from the bench were carried out.

"If I wired the governor," Worden said finally, "I'd have to turn my star in. Maybe I won't run again, but as long as I am sheriff, I'll do my job without help from the outside." He picked up his pipe and filled it, then added, "If you'd set the date the morning after the trial, we wouldn't be in this shape, Judge."

"I had to give time for an appeal," Webb said quietly. "You never hang a man the day after he's convicted."

"Wouldn't make any difference anyhow," Quinn added. "The squeeze is on us now because time is running out. It would have been the same if the Judge had set the date then."

Webb rose. "All right, Bill, but I'll tell you this. You'll live to regret the decision you just made."

Worden, in his anger, had forgotten about George Ballard and Ellen, and now, remembering them, his anger returned. He said harshly, "There's been talk about me not doing my job on account of Ballard and Ellen. If you're thinking that . . ."

"We're not thinking anything of the kind." Doc Quinn got up and put his derby on his head. "Duty has always been a fetish with you. It always will be, regardless of what it costs you or your family, but you might give some thought to this. What will Ellen say if you shoot George tonight?"

Worden said nothing. What could he say? That possibility had been in the back of his mind, but he had not worried about it. Ballard was not the man his grandfather had been. Or his father. Jiggs Larribee and the rest of Ballard's crew might be in on the trouble, but not Ballard.

Webb walked to the door, then turned. "There's one other thing you should know. Preacher Rigdon and a bunch of farmer women are in the church having a prayer meeting."

There was something ludicrous in the idea of the law being afraid of the prayers of Preacher Rigdon and a bunch of farmer women. He said, "If you think I'm worried about any thunderbolts the Lord is going to throw . . ."

"I was thinking about what will happen tonight," Webb said stiffly. "After the women have gone home and their husbands have come to church. I understand that is what they plan."

Webb and Quinn left then. Worden lighted his pipe, doubts beginning to work in him. Suppose he was killed tonight? What would Ada and Ellen do? There was very little money in the bank, and Kirby was too young and irresponsible to support them. There would just be the house and it wouldn't sell for much, not with property the way it was in Gunlock.

But there was George Ballard. Worden pulled

on his pipe as he teetered back and forth in his chair. Ballard would look out for them. Worden's death would simply make Ellen's and Ballard's marriage certain.

Worden's mind turned back to the thought he'd had about Ballard a moment before. He had not faced up to this before. He had never actually accused Ballard of being a coward, not even in his own mind, but indirectly that was what he had done when Doc Quinn had asked him what Ellen would say if he shot Ballard. Then he wondered if he was judging Ballard by his lights and not by Ellen's.

He got up and put on his hat. A hell of a thing, he thought, when a man's personal problems got mixed up with his official ones. Ada would understand, but Ellen wouldn't, if it came to the final breaking point with Ballard. She would hate him all of her life.

He left the courthouse and started down Main Street toward Preacher Rigdon's church. He could clear up one thing at least. Rigdon was a fanatic, a zealot who was certain that he had his own pipeline to God, and everyone, including John Harris, was lost if he wasn't in Rigdon's private fold. But whatever the preacher's faults were, lying was not among them. If the farmers had any intention of lynching Lake before the legal hour of execution, Rigdon would say so.

The temperature had dropped, and the black clouds that had boiled up around Red Mountain had worked out across the sky and now almost covered it. A damp wind came down off the mountains. It had rained somewhere up there in the foothills, washing the sage, and now the air was sharp with a pungent, tangy odor. This happened several times every summer, always reminding Worden of Thanksgiving and the sharply scented smell of Ada's kitchen.

As he passed the hotel, two men ran out of the lobby, one of them calling, "Sheriff." City men, he saw, reporters from Denver. One of them, Sid Lesser, had been here for Lake's trial. Worden had not seen the other one.

"Just wanted to get a story on the wire tonight," Lesser said. "About the execution in the morning. We'd like to quote you."

"We sure would," the other man said. "I'm Fred DeLong. I've been wanting to meet you, Sheriff."

DeLong held out his hand and Worden gave it a perfunctory grip. He was young, not much more than a kid, and eager. Too eager. Worden said, "I've just one thing to say. The execution will take place. And don't come around the courthouse because you won't be permitted to see Lake."

"Now look here, Sheriff . . ." Lesser began.

"No looking here about it," Worden snapped. "You show up in the courthouse and start making a racket about seeing Lake, and so help me, I'll throw you into a cell for disturbing the peace."

He wheeled and went on, hearing Lesser mutter in disgust, "There's your cow-country tin star for you. They think they're cousins to the Almighty every time."

Worden's teeth clenched. He felt like going back and cracking their heads together, but he knew he wouldn't gain anything. He didn't stop until he reached the corner, and when he looked back, they had disappeared. But he saw something else that held him there. Jiggs Larribee was riding into town.

Worden moved around the corner and stood so he could see Larribee, but probably would not be seen himself. The Lazy B foreman rode leisurely, looking neither to the right nor left. A tough, arrogant man, Jiggs Larribee, and a good cowman who was held to George Ballard by bonds of loyalty that went back to the days of old Longhorn who had taught Larribee all he knew about the cattle business.

This was the quality in George Ballard that made him dangerous. He was always on the edge of things, always out of reach but holding tight to the reins. By paying Larribee well and giving him his head, he had to all intents and purposes made the foreman a partner in the Lazy B, and Worden had no doubt Larribee would carry out Ballard's orders without question.

Worden waited until Larribee racked his horse and went into the bank. He had come for his instructions, Worden thought, the first man to ride in off the range all day. Lew Hogan and Jess

Ryman and the rest of the little fry had not made an appearance. Larribee was the go-between, making sure what Ballard wanted done. The others would follow his lead.

Worden went on down the street to Rigdon's church. It was a plain white structure squatting here at the edge of town, no bell or cross or decoration of any kind, just a square, graceless building that was symbolic of Preacher Rigdon's brand of gospel.

The church building was surrounded by buggies, buckboards, and wagons just as it was every Sunday morning and evening. When Worden was a block away, he heard the singing, but it was different than it was on Sunday. No bass or tenor. Women's voices, high and shrill, and a little off key.

He took off his hat and went in. He stood in the back, suddenly realizing that it would be difficult to talk to Rigdon, that this might go on for hours. The pews were almost filled with women and children. A red-headed girl was playing the organ, and Rigdon, standing beside his pulpit, was beating time with a big hand. If he saw Worden come in, he gave no sign.

Rigdon was a short man, heavy-muscled and inordinately wide of shoulder. By reputation, he was the strongest man in Grant County, and some of the stories told about his strength were fantastic. Like the time one of his elders, a man named Orson, had had a heavily loaded wagon fall on him, and Rigdon, alone with the man, had

92

lifted the wagon so Orson had been able to crawl free.

Doc Quinn patched Orson up and returned to town, shaking his head. "I saw that wagon," Quinn said. "It would take three ordinary men and a mule to lift it, but Orson swears the preacher did it himself. With the Lord's help, of course."

There were other stories that drifted in from the outside, stories that Rigdon denied. About his wild youth in San Francisco before he had been saved when he'd been a prize fighter and had killed a man with his fists. They might be lies, Worden thought, but he had no doubt Rigdon could have done it.

When they finished the hymn, Rigdon raised a hand and tilting his head back, looked up while everyone else but Worden bowed their heads. "Lord of Hosts," Rigdon prayed, "come to the aid of Thy people. Lord of Abraham and Isaac and Jacob, Lord of David who was victorious because Thy hand was with him, hear us. Thy people in the time of our need. Strike down our enemies. Place the rope upon the murderer's neck and stretch it and burn his soul in eternal hell."

He went on in his great voice, and Worden thought about John Harris who seemed to worship another God, a God of love and forgiveness, a God who made the rain fall upon both the just and the unjust. Were there two Gods in heaven? It was enough to make a man wonder.

Worden felt a tug at his coat sleeve. He had not noticed Mrs. Lyle leave her pew and come to him. He looked at her and saw her jerk her head toward the door, so he backed through it and permitted her to lead him to the corner of the building.

Mrs. Lyle was a small, hot-tempered woman who would have been a good mate for Jeannie Mason's mother in everything but size. Pound for pound, he thought, Mrs. Lyle was a better man than Mrs. Mason had ever been.

"Why did you come here and break into our service?" Mrs. Lyle whispered accusingly. "Didn't you feel the presence of the Holy Ghost and know that you were defiling a place of worship?"

"Can't say I did," Worden murmured. "I want to talk to the preacher. How long will it last?"

"It may be hours," she said. "Go away."

He might just as well. He met her hot eyes, bitter with indignation at his intrusion. He said, "I heard that your men were coming tonight after work. Is that true?"

"It's true. And don't you try to stop them. We know all about you and the way you feel about that murderer and about your girl and Ballard. If you try . . ."

He turned and walked away. So it was true. If the cowmen came, they would go to the Casino and drink themselves into a state of courage, but the farmers would come to church.

The sun was buried by the black clouds, and

94

thunder made a distant rumble behind him. The light was thin and a little eerie. He looked down at the star on his shirt. Just a piece of metal with no shine to it. Did it mean anything, he asked himself, anything at all?

# *Chapter Seven*

**WHEN** George Ballard returned to town after seeing Nan Hogan, he left his team and buggy at the livery stable and went at once to the bank.

It was not until he had closed the door in his private office that he realized he had missed his noon meal. His housekeeper would be furious because he had not told her he was leaving town and would not go home for dinner. Well, it was too late now, so he'd let it go until evening.

He lighted a cigar. He wasn't hungry anyhow. Something he'd had for breakfast must have disagreed with him. His stomach was queasy. If he had eaten dinner, he probably wouldn't have kept it down.

He dropped into his chair at his desk, thinking about his housekeeper and wondering why he was scared of her. She liked order and routine: she kept the big house clean and cooked good meals and saw to it that his clothes were in order. He would find no better housekeeper in Grant County. Still, he would have to apologize to her tonight, and the prospect irritated him.

He'd be glad when he was married. Ellen could keep her or let her go as she pleased. If she kept the woman, it would be up to her to placate her, and Ballard would be relieved of the bowing and scraping which was not fitting for a man in his position.

He leaned back in his chair and closed his eyes, the droning of a fly against the window lulling him almost to sleep. He would be married in a little over two weeks. He began thinking about his wedding night and desire grew in him. It had been a long time since he'd had a woman. He could not afford to risk the gossip that would follow if he went to one of the girls who lived over the Casino, and he had not been in Denver since before Christmas.

If Ellen was like Nan . . . ! No, he wouldn't be marrying her if she was. He had never intended marrying Nan. A man could find pleasure in a loose woman, but when it came to marriage, he looked for someone like Ellen.

Then a startling thought occurred to him. He finished his cigar and started another one, turning the idea over in his mind. He didn't want to stay in town tonight because he didn't want to be here at nine o'clock in the morning, but he had been unable to think of an excuse to leave.

Now he wondered if he could persuade Ellen to leave with him tonight on the eight o'clock train and be married in Denver. They wouldn't have the big church wedding Ellen was counting on. But Ballard had the feeling it was Mrs. Worden more than Ellen who was planning it.

Another thing had been bothering Ballard. Bill Worden did not entirely approve of him as a son-in-law. Not that Worden had ever said so. It was one of those intangibles a man feels, a lack of cordiality on Worden's part.

Ballard had often wondered about it. He was sure he had never given Worden any reason to dislike him. Perhaps it went back to the old days when the sheriffs had been pawns in the hands of the Ballard men.

Although he had never tried to dictate Worden's policy, the thought might be in the sheriff's mind that he would try after he married into the family. Or it might be some of this talk about Ed Lake and the cattlemen's association.

Ballard got up and began pacing the floor, the queasiness returning to his stomach. In an effort to keep out of Lake's jail break, he had handed Nan Hogan a club she could use. He had given her the hundred dollars; he had emphasized the idea that she was saving Lew's neck, and he warned her he would deny having any part in the jail break.

He had tried to cover all bets, but it might have been better if he had gone to Jeannie Mason and left Nan out of it. She had plenty of reason to hate him. And she did, judging by the way she had welcomed him that morning.

Oh, Nan had said she was happy with Lew, but that was probably her pride talking. He had found her working like a man, and his sudden appearance had probably reminded her of the promise he had made and failed to keep.

He swore and threw his cigar stub into the spittoon at the corner of his desk. No, he was better off if he got out of town until after the hanging, and he thought he had a good chance of talking Ellen into going with him.

A knock on the door broke into his thoughts. Probably Brown wanting to know if he should make a loan. Ballard called irritably, "Come in."

But it was Jiggs Larribee who opened the door and came in. He said, "Howdy, Mr. Ballard," and closed the door.

"Sit down, Jiggs."

Ballard was relieved; then the queasiness was in his stomach again and the relief was gone. Larribee seldom came to town to see him, and judging from his foreman's taciturn face, something was wrong. Ballard sat down at his desk.

Jiggs Larribee was considerably older than Ballard, a tall, long-boned man who had all the marks of a cowman upon him, even to the traditional bowed legs. He had a good pair of shoulders, big hands and heavy wrists and, winter or summer, his face was the mahogany brown that constant exposure to wind and sun puts upon a man.

Larribee had been trained by Longhorn Ballard. Loyalty had been a dominant trait in the old man, and he had instilled that same trait in Larribee, a loyalty not only to his ranch and employer, but to a way of life. To Longhorn all men had been divided into two classes: friends of the stockmen and enemies of stockmen, and no room for anyone between. Jiggs Larribee felt the same way.

Ballard lit a cigar and waited while Larribee rolled and sealed a cigarette, then touched a match flame to it. Larribee took his time about everything. Ballard was often irritated by this slowness, but he knew his foreman too well to try to hurry him.

Finally Larribee tilted his Stetson back with a bony thumb, gray eyes fixed on Ballard. He asked, and this direct approach was typical of him, "What are we going to do about Ed Lake?"

"Nothing," Ballard said. "He had a fair trial."

Larribee leaned back in his chair, the cigarette dangling loosely from one corner of his mouth, the smoke drifting upward across his face. He said without raising his voice, "You're wrong, Mr. Ballard, we will do something."

Ballard shook his head. "There was a time when we could have, but that day died with my grandfather."

Larribee kept looking at him. Ballard never knew what was behind those gray eyes. Not once had Larribee raised his voice to him, or argued with him about anything since he had inherited the Lazy B. The foreman knew his place and he knew his job, and he never forgot either. But now Larribee had reached the point where he was going to argue, and Ballard knew he was in a squeeze before Larribee started.

"I ain't an owner," Larribee said, "so I don't belong to the association. I never went to one of your meetings, but I've heard the talk same as everybody else. Maybe it's true. Maybe it ain't.

But one thing's sure. Three men were shot who settled on Lazy B range. Now I ain't defending Ed Lake for the way he done the shooting, if he did all three of 'em. But it had to be done, one way or the other, or we were finished."

"It happens that our range includes a ten-mile stretch along the creek," Ballard said. "If it had belonged to any of the others, the farmers would have settled there just the same."

"But it was Lazy B grass," Larribee said in the same deceptively soft voice. "If Lake hadn't done what he did, we'd have hundreds of 'em on our grass by now. Everyone of them sodbusters south of the creek has got brothers and cousins, and all them brothers and cousins would be plowing up our grass if they thought they'd live long enough to see a crop."

"You sound like Lew Hogan."

Larribee nodded. "But I was thinking like Lew a long time ago. He came over this morning. He rode over again after dinner with Jess Ryman. They want to know what the Lazy B is gonna do."

"Nothing," Ballard said.

Larribee dropped his cigarette stub into the spittoon. He said, "Mr. Ballard, I ain't a killer. If it had been me, I never would have sent for Ed Lake. I'd found some other way to do the job, but he was sent for and he done what he was supposed to do, and now we've got to get him out of jail."

Ballard rose and walked to a window. You

couldn't argue with simple-minded men like Lew Hogan and Jiggs Larribee. Simple! That was the word. They simplified every issue. Just the way old Longhorn used to do. He'd have taken the jail apart before now and thumbed his nose at Bill Worden. But Worden hadn't been sheriff when Longhorn was alive.

"What does Lew figure on doing?" Ballard asked.

"He's got a scheme that I think will work," Larribee said. "A couple of 'em will go upstairs to the jail a little before sunup and talk to Mac. Or Worden if he's there. Just ask about Lake. You know, act friendly as if they wanted to help if anything was wrong."

Larribee rolled another cigarette. "Then the rest of the boys who will be wearing masks will come in and throw their guns on everybody. There'll be a mix up, and the two who were there first will bump into Worden and Mac. Won't take more'n a second or two, but it'll be long enough to crack Mac and Worden on the head. Then they'll let Lake out. Nobody can identify the boys with the masks and the first two will claim they got boogered. Worden won't have no cause to arrest 'em."

It might work, Ballard thought, but Worden being the man he was, would fight, and if he didn't get killed, he'd work on it until he had all of them in jail.

"Let them do it if they want to," Ballard said finally. "We're staying out of it. For one thing, the Ballard name must be protected. And we can't afford to get the bank involved in it."

"I figured you might look at it that way." Larribee made no effort to hide his scorn. "I reckon you'd best start looking for a new ramrod."

"No," Ballard said quickly. "You've got a good job, Jiggs. And I need you."

He hesitated, realizing that Larribee had made his decision before he had left the Lazy B. To most men this would not be worth a quarrel, but to Jiggs Larribee it was part of his way of life that went back to his boyhood when he'd worked for Longhorn. There was a quality in Larribee that would not let him change.

"No," Larribee said. "This is the end of the line."

Larribee would have got up if Timothy Brown hadn't knocked on the door, calling, "Mr. Ballard, Jeannie Mason is out here to see you and she won't go away."

"I'm busy. Tell her to come back tomorrow."

"I already told her, but she says if you won't see her, she'll kick the lid off. I don't know what she means, but that's what she says."

Ballard swore. Nan had bungled this. Or Lew had. Maybe Nan had taken the hundred dollars and had not said anything to Lew. Or Jeannie.

"Stay here, Jiggs," Ballard said. "I'll just be a minute."

"No use wasting your time," Larribee said.

"You wait," Ballard snapped. "I'm not quite

as lacking in my sense of obligation as you and Hogan think. There's a better way to do this."

Ballard opened the door, knowing that Larribee would stay. Jeannie Mason was standing in the front of the bank, defiant eyes on Ballard as he pushed back the gate at the end of the counter and walked to her.

"I told you this morning . . ." Ballard began.

"I know what you told me, but everything is different now," Jeannie said. "Nan Hogan brought me the gun and told me what you planned for us to do. It's a very good plan and I'm sure it will work."

He stared at her pale face, mentally cursing Nan and knowing he had made a bigger mistake going to her than he had realized. He said hotly, "I didn't give Mrs. Hogan a gun, and I will not turn a hand to save Ed Lake's neck."

"You're not a very good liar," Jeannie said. "My mother used to say the Ballard blood had run thin in the third generation. I guess this is what she meant. You're afraid to admit even to me what you've done and what you want done."

"Get out," Ballard breathed. "I have never laid a hand on a woman, but I will now if you don't leave."

"I won't go until I get what I came for," Jeannie said stubbornly. "My money's gone. Both Ed and I will need some. When I see him tonight, we'll decide where to meet. I will never be able to come back here, so I want to sell my house. Or give you a mortgage on it. I think five hundred dollars will be enough."

He could not believe this was Jeannie Mason, stubborn and defiant and sure of herself. Then he thought: *Why not give it to her? It would be worth five hundred dollars to get her out of town.*

He said, "I don't have time to see Judge Webb and have him draw up the papers, but I'll give you the money on your personal note."

"Thank you," she said as if she had been sure he would not refuse. "Do you want the key to my house?"

"No. You may decide to come back, and if you do, you'll need your house. When are you leaving?"

"On the eight o'clock train, but I won't be back. Do whatever you need to do to get title to my place."

Ballard swung around and slamming the gate back, went through it. He said, "Timothy, Miss Mason wants to borrow five hundred dollars. Give her a note to sign and let her have the money."

Brown's pale brows lifted in a questioning arc. "Mr. Ballard, it has been our policy . . ."

"I know the policy of my own bank," Ballard snapped. "Miss Mason's mother's credit was always good and I'm sure hers is. Let her have the money."

"Yes sir," Brown said.

Ballard returned to his office and shut the door. He said, "Jiggs, there's always a dozen ways to skin a cat. The problem isn't getting the cat skinned. It's picking the right method, and raiding the jail and running the chance of having some men killed is not the right way. Now you go back to the Lazy B and stay there. Don't ever say anything again about me looking for a new ramrod."

Larribee sat there, blinking slowly, gray eyes pinned on Ballard's face. Finally he said, "How do you aim to skin the cat?"

"It'd be better if you didn't know," Ballard said, "but I promise you that the cat will be skinned." Still Larribee sat there, and slowly the realization came to Ballard that the man did not believe him. He added, "I'll tell you if you won't pass it on to the others. Just tell them to keep out of it. Lake will have a gun in his hands tonight. The plans are already made."

Larribee gave it some thought. His dark face showed nothing, but Ballard knew he was being torn between what he considered an obligation and his sense of loyalty to the Lazy B and his employer. Finally the loyalty won.

Larribee rose. "All right, Mr. Ballard. I should of knowed you'd take care of it. Sorry I bothered you."

He went out. Ballard sat down at his desk, his knees buckling under him. For the first time since his father had died, his judgment had been openly questioned. Brown had tried to tell him how to run his bank, and he wasn't sure Larribee was entirely satisfied.

He glanced at his watch. It was time to close

106

the bank. He had to get out of here, had to breathe some fresh air. He had to see Ellen. He swore as he got up and put on his hat. He needed her trust, her belief that he could do no wrong, and it bothered him to realize how great that need was.

As he passed Brown, he said, "I'm going home, Timothy. You can lock up."

"Yes sir," Brown said, his eyes not meeting Ballard's.

Outside the air was damp and penetrating. Ballard shivered as he glanced along the empty street and cursed a country where the weather changed the way it did here. It was going to rain. Well, the range was dry. The rain would be good for the grass, but why did it have to turn so damned cold?

As he climbed the hill to the Worden house, he wondered why he stayed in Gunlock. He'd have a fortune if he sold out. Not a big one, but enough for him and Ellen to be comfortable the rest of their lives. He'd ask her how she'd like to live in California.

He rang the Worden door bell, hoping he wouldn't make Ellen angry by calling at this hour. Usually he dropped in after supper unless he had arrangements to take her for a buggy ride.

But when she opened the door, he saw the quick pleasure that filled her blue eyes. No other woman, not even Nan, had ever looked at him the way Ellen did. It was a source of never-ending wonder to him. She loved him, and she wanted him to know by every gesture and glance she gave him that she did.

"Come in, George," she said. "I was hoping you'd drop in on your way home."

He stepped into the hall and she closed the door, then she was in his arms, holding him hard as if afraid he would somehow escape her. She tilted her face upward for his kiss, and in that moment all the fear and worry and uncertainty that had been in him this day was gone.

She drew her head back. "George, stay for supper. It's going to be late tonight because we have been working all day on my dress. Daddy won't be home, so we'll have to eat alone if you don't stay."

He hesitated, thinking about his housekeeper who probably was cooking his supper now. Ellen whispered, "Please, George."

From somewhere in the back of the house, Mrs. Worden called, "Is that George, Ellen?"

"Yes, he's going to stay for supper." She lowered her voice. "You are, aren't you, George?"

He couldn't very well say no. He said, "Sure I'll stay."

Mrs. Worden came along the hall, wiping her hands on her apron. The light was thin, but Ballard noticed as he had so many times how closely she resembled Ellen. He said, "You certainly have the secret of youth, Mrs. Worden. You and Ellen look like twins."

She was pleased, and Ballard thought that probably Worden never said things like that to her. He was not an articulate man about matters that were emotionally important to him.

"You have a talent for saying nice things, George," Mrs. Worden said. "Just for that I'll bake you a chocolate cake."

"I couldn't ask for anything better," Ballard said. "I'll go home and change my clothes; then I'll come back."

"We'll eat about seven," Mrs. Worden said.

She returned to the kitchen, and Ballard took Ellen's hands. He said in a low tone, "I had an idea this afternoon, honey, and it's got me so excited I can't think straight. Let's take the eight o'clock train and go to Denver. We'll be married in the morning and I'll give you the best honeymoon a girl ever had."

Startled, she tipped her head back and looked at him. "George, that's crazy. After all our plans for a church wedding, and the work we've put on my dress. I couldn't. I just couldn't."

He squeezed her hands. "Ellen, I love you. I guess I'm afraid something will happen."

"That's crazy, too. What could happen?"

"Oh, I don't know. It's just that I love you so much I can't wait. I've been thinking about it all afternoon. Waiting two weeks is just wasting time when we could be together."

She said hesitantly, "Mamma would have a fit. She didn't have a big wedding when she married Daddy, and she's got her heart set on giving me a fancy one."

"She'll understand," he said.

"I . . . I guess she would." Ellen laughed shakily. "But I don't know. Let me think about it."

He kissed her, knowing he could not press for a decision now. She'd do it, he thought. He opened the door and stood there a moment, his eyes on her face. He said, "Every time I look at you, I thank God that this happened to me. I don't know how or why it did, but I'm not one to question Providence."

He swung around, leaving her standing there, and walked rapidly down the path to the sidewalk. He began to whistle. Everything was going to be all right, he told himself. Everything. He wouldn't be here at nine o'clock in the morning. Running away with Ellen gave him a logical excuse for being out of town when they hanged Ed Lake. But she would never know why he didn't want to wait. There was a good chance Lake would get away, but Worden was a hard man to fool, and Ballard wasn't one to gamble.

# Chapter Eight

JEANNIE Mason almost grabbed the money out of Timothy Brown's reluctant hands as soon as she signed the note. She ran out of the bank without as much as a "Thank you." No one deserved thanking. Brown had given her the money only because he had been told to, and Ballard had let her have it because she had him in a squeeze and he knew it.

There was a good deal of her mother in her at this moment. She hated all men except Ed Lake. There was only one way to get what you wanted out of them. That was to be stronger than they were, and to use that strength ruthlessly and brutally until you got what you were after. She had done that with George Ballard. Her mother would have approved, she thought.

As soon as she entered her house, she felt the heat from the early part of the day that had been retained within the walls of the living room; she smelled the baking pie and knew that Nan had a roaring fire in the range that was adding to the heat. When she went into the kitchen, she saw that Nan was keeping the oven open.

Nan, red-faced and sweating, smiled ruefully at Jeannie. "I had completely forgotten how to bake in a good oven," she said. "The old range I have is so burned out I have to get a terrific fire going just to bake biscuits." She pointed to the open oven. "Now I've got to watch this pie like a baby."

But Jeannie, hardly half listening, threw the roll of greenbacks on the table. "I've got it, Nan. Look. I've got it."

Nan glanced at the money and brought her eyes to Jeannie's excited face. "Honey, if I didn't know you, I'd say you were a bank robber."

"I am, sort of," Jeannie said, and told her what she'd done.

Nan put her hands on her wide hips and gave Jeannie a look of frank admiration. "I wish I could have seen George's face. And Tim Brown's. He never lets a penny slip through his fingers without squeezing it so hard the Indian whoops." She bent down to look into the oven. "Guess I'd better get that pie out of there. It's a little burned around the edge now."

Jeannie sank into a chair at the table. She hadn't eaten all day and she began to tremble. She said, "As soon as I rest, I'll get supper. I don't feel like eating, but I guess I'd better."

"You sit right there," Nan said. "I'll fix something. I'll bet you haven't had anything to eat all day."

"No," Jeannie admitted, "I haven't."

Her conscience made her uneasy. She should get up and help Nan, but she felt utterly washed out, so she sat at the table, watching Nan carry the pie into the pantry. Jeannie had admired Nan when she'd run the restaurant, particularly her strength and her indifference to the gossip about her.

Now Nan moved from kitchen to pantry and back again with as much efficiency as if she had worked here for months. She made coffee and set the table, fried ham and eggs, and brought bread and butter from the pantry.

"Sure nice to work in a real kitchen," Nan said. "I don't suppose we'll ever have enough money to build a decent house and live like this." She wiped her sweaty face with her apron. "Not that I'm kicking. I wouldn't be in this mess if I didn't want to keep what I've got."

"Nan, I just thought of something," Jeannie said worriedly. "I told Ballard I was taking the eight o'clock train, but I can't. If this doesn't work . . ."

Nan was pouring coffee. "You stop right there." She tipped the pot back and glared at Jeannie. "In the first place, it will work. In the second place, you told George you'd go. And in the third place, you've got to be out of town when it comes off." Nan carried the coffee pot back to the stove. "Don't you worry about me doing my part. I'll see that Ed gets the gun."

They ate in silence, Nan with hearty hunger, Jeannie because she thought she should, and when they had finished, she said, "Nan, I told Ballard to take the house, but I didn't say he could have the furniture. You get Lew to bring a wagon and take everything home you can use.

There's the stove for one thing. And I've got lots of bedding. Some nice dishes. Just take anything you want."

Shocked, Nan said, "I couldn't do that. You might come back someday."

"I'll never come back," Jeannie said fiercely, "and you know why I can't."

"No," Nan said. "I guess you can't."

Jeannie got up and went into her bedroom. She was rested now, but she felt her blood pounding through her body. So much depended on how she handled herself at the jail, and it was nearly time to go. She found paper and pen and ink; she wrote out a bill of sale for everything that was in the house and went back to the kitchen.

"I guess you're right about me leaving town on the eight o'clock," she said. "Worden will think I gave Ed the gun and he'd put me in jail. I couldn't bear that. I don't know where Ed will tell me to meet him, but wherever it is, I want to get there ahead of him."

Nan stared at the bill of sale, then raised her eyes to Jeannie. She said softly, "You don't need to do this."

"I want to. It's all I can do, Nan." She bit her lip, and added impulsively, "You don't know how it's been to talk to a woman again."

Nan rose. "That pie's cooled off by now. I'll wrap a dishcloth around it." She hesitated, then put an arm around Jeannie's slim waist and hugged her. "You're good, Jeannie. Don't let the way these sanctimonious old hens have treated you make anything else out of you."

She went into the pantry and returned with the pie, a dishcloth wrapped around it. "You'd better start. That string will be soaked with cherry juice, but it'll still work."

Jeannie took the pie and left the house. As she walked down the hill toward the courthouse, she shivered a little, for the wind was heavy with the promise of rain, and the clouds were so thick and black that the light was strained thin, giving the impression that twilight was at hand.

When she reached the courthouse, she was no longer afraid. She knew exactly what she had to do. She spoke to Orval Jones who was sweeping the lower hall. He gave her a half-inch nod and went on sweeping. She climbed the stairs, smiling. No one would suspect her of helping Ed break jail, she thought. She wasn't important enough to suspect.

Worden was not in his office. She went on along the hall to the jail, and was relieved to find him there. McNamara was not around. She said breathlessly, "I brought it, Mr. Worden. I hope he hasn't had his supper."

Worden rose from where he had been sitting at the desk and watched her unwrap the pie. "Smells good." He gave her a long look, searching her pale face, then took the pie and weighed it in his hand. Some of the juice had run out, making a sticky syrup on the bottom of the pan. He set the pie on the desk and wiped his hands on the dishcloth. "No, he hasn't had his supper. Mac's getting it from the hotel now."

She watched him take a knife out of his pocket and open it, and for one long, terrible second she could not breathe. *He knows,* she thought. All her hopes and plans had failed. Then, as he reached for the pie, the open knife in his other hand, the panic left her and her mind began to function.

"Don't cut it." She leaped toward him and snatched the pie from the desk and backed away. "Mr. Worden, isn't it enough to hang him? Do you have to do this, too?"

He looked at her gravely. "I wasn't going to eat it, if that's what you're worrying about."

She moved back another step, holding the pie so tightly that her thumbs pressed into the flaky crust. "Mr. Worden, I'll never see Ed again. I'm leaving town on the eight o'clock train." She swallowed, her lips quivering. "It's the last thing I'll ever be able to give him. I . . . I'd like for him to cut it."

Worden closed the knife and dropped it into his pocket. "I guess it will be all right. I'd have to cut it if it was a cake, but you couldn't very well bake a gun in a cherry pie, could you?"

She didn't answer. She hugged the pie to her, watching him pick up his ring of keys and unlock the heavy door that led into the corridor. "Come along," he said, and held the door open for her. She went through it and waited for him to go on and unlock Ed's cell.

"You've got a visitor," Worden said. "Stay

116

over there where you are."

Dealing with men like Ed Lake for eleven years had developed a strong sense of caution in Worden. Lake remained on his bunk while Worden unlocked the cell door and taking the pie from Jeannie, laid it down inside, then closed the door and locked it.

"Save your dessert," Worden said. "Mac's gone after your supper." He nodded at Jeannie. "You can have your visit now. Just keep your hands on this side of the bars."

Worden stepped back. Jeannie pressed her face against the cold bars. She said softly, "Ed." There was one more thing she had to do. She stood with her left side to Worden. She had made a roll of half the money, gripping it tightly in her right hand. Now she dropped it and nudged it between the bars with her foot.

Worden was watching, but he was too far away to hear what she said. Lake came to her, and here in the gloom with his back to the cell window, she could not see his face clearly, but she sensed that the cold confidence which had marked him from the first was not in him now.

He saw the money and placed a foot upon it. She whispered, "I got five hundred dollars from Ballard. I'm giving you half of it. I'll use the rest to go to wherever you want to meet me."

"Expect me to fly out of here?" he asked bitterly. "What's that damned Ballard done?"

"Enough. Now listen. There's some twine in the bottom of the pie. At ten o'clock tonight let it out of the window. Have you got anything to weigh the end down?"

"I'll find something."

"Nan Hogan has a gun. She'll tie it to the end and all you have to do is to pull it back. There's no moon tonight and we're going to have a storm. It'll be too dark for anyone to see her."

"Well, by God, a gun," Lake whispered. "So old Lew's taking care of me."

"It was Ballard's idea. Where will I meet you?"

"Santa Fe. Won't take me long to get there, neither."

"What will you do for a horse?"

"I'll pick one off the hitch pole. If it rains, they won't have no tracks to follow. It'll work slick as goose grease."

"I've got to go, Ed," she breathed. "Kiss me."

"Hold on. My valise still in the hotel room?"

"I guess so. Why?"

One of the first things she had done after his arrest was to pay his room rent for months ahead. It had seemed a foolish waste of money, but he'd insisted, and Worden had agreed to leave his clothes in the hotel room, accepting Lake's explanation that he'd need them when some higher authority freed him.

"There's a false bottom in my valise," he said. "Take it home and rip the bottom out. My money's there."

Lake pressed his face against the bars. Jeannie kissed him, closing her eyes, her hands pressed hard against her sides. She wanted so much to put her arms around him, to feel his arms around her, but she couldn't risk disobeying Worden's orders.

She drew back, whispering, "I love you, Ed. Don't ever forget that."

"It's the one good thing I have to remember," he said. Then he called, "Sheriff, I've got a favor to ask."

Worden moved forward to stand beside Jeannie. "What is it?"

Jeannie retreated across the corridor. Terrified, she told herself that this was a mistake. Worden would see the money if Ed forgot and moved his foot.

"I want Jeannie to have my horse and saddle," Lake said. "And I've got some things in my hotel room. I want her to have them, too."

"We can draw up a will," Worden said, "but she said she was leaving town tonight."

"Well, just give her permission to get my valise out of the hotel. You can do that without no will."

"All right." Worden jerked his head at Jeannie. "Come on."

She was crying as she followed Worden down the corridor and into the office. She waited beside the desk while Worden wrote a note to Marv Tremaine. Tremaine lived in town; he had bought the hotel after selling his ranch to Jess Ryman.

Worden folded the note and handed it to

Jeannie. "I'm sorry for you," he said. "Not for Lake, though."

"You're wrong about him, Mr. Worden." Jeannie wiped her eyes. "Everybody is. He's always been good to me. I don't believe he did what people say he did."

She whirled and ran out of the room, almost bumping into McNamara who was coming in with a tray that held Lake's supper. The deputy said, "How are you, Jeannie?" She hurried past him, not speaking to him. There was so little time left to do the things she had to do.

As she left the courthouse, she thought about Worden who had been kind to her. And McNamara. She had nothing against either of them. They might be killed before the night was over. She would blame herself for it, but it was too late now. Then she felt better when she thought that Ed would not fire the gun. A shot would alarm the town. He'd just use it to bluff his way out of jail.

She hurried to the hotel. Lightning was working across the sky with snapping fingers of flame, and the rumble of thunder seemed very close. She hoped the rain would hold off for a few hours. It might mean the difference between escape and failure for Ed.

Marv Tremaine was behind the desk when Jeannie went into the lobby. He said, "Evening, Jeannie," his tone courteous. His wife would not be that polite, she thought. Mrs. Worden and Ellen wouldn't be, either.

She gave Worden's note to Tremaine. "I'm leaving town tonight," she said. "Ed wanted me to have his things."

Tremaine read the note and scratched his long nose. He looked at Jeannie, scratched his nose again, and read the note a second time. "No sense to this," he muttered. "Nothing in Lake's room but a suitcase full of clothes. Bill's been through 'em half a dozen times."

"I want them," she pleaded. "You don't care, do you?"

"I sure don't." Tremaine studied the note again. "Looks like Bill's writing, all right, though why he'd let you have 'em I dunno. Well, you wait here. I'll fetch the valise down."

It seemed to her he was gone an hour. She walked restlessly around the room, wanting to scream for him to hurry. She kept looking at the cuckoo clock on the wall. The big hand seemed stuck. It was not yet seven, but she still had to pack her things.

Presently Tremaine came down the stairs, moving with irritating slowness, the leather valise in his right hand. "I went through the bureau drawers again just to be sure," he said, "but there wasn't nothing but some socks and stuff like that. I sure don't savvy this. Lake didn't have no clothes when he got here but what he was wearing, then he went out and bought this valise . . ."

Jeannie took the valise from him. "Thank you, Mr. Tremaine," she said, and ran out of the lobby, leaving him staring after her, completely puzzled.

She was out of breath when she reached home. Nan had finished the dishes and had lighted a lamp. When Jeannie came in, Nan said, "I could have packed your things if I'd thought to ask you what you wanted to take." She saw the valise then. "Did you buy that? I thought you had . . ."

"It's Ed's. I got it from the hotel."

Jeannie ran past Nan into the kitchen and laid the valise on the table. She got a butcher knife from the pantry and returning to the table, called, "Bring the lamp, Nan. It's awfully dark for this time of year."

"It's those clouds," Nan said, and picking up the lamp from the living room table, carried it into the kitchen.

Jeannie opened the valise and dumped the clothes on the floor. She began hacking at the bottom. Nan demanded, "Have you gone mad, Jeannie?" Then she said something under her breath, for Jeannie had cut a corner of the false bottom and with a frantic jerk, ripped it out. There, laid out in long rows, were more green-backs than either Jeannie or Nan had ever seen before in their lives.

For a moment both women stared at the money, then Jeannie remembered the gossip that Ed had been paid well for the killings. She looked at Nan, and knew the same thought was in her mind.

"It's his poker winnings," Jeannie cried. "He

told me about his big games."

"Then why did he hide it?" Nan asked.

"I don't know." Jeannie realized she was screaming. Then she added, lowering her voice, "It doesn't make any difference. That's how he got it, I tell you."

She picked up the money with trembling fingers. A sheet of writing paper fluttered to the floor, but she didn't bother to look at it. "I've got to catch that train," she said. "Bring the lamp and help me. Please."

She ran into the bedroom, holding the wad of money with both hands. She had no time to think about this. She had to hurry, had to get away. But when she looked at Nan who was coming into the bedroom with the lamp, she saw something in the other woman's face she didn't like.

"Nan, you'll do what you promised, won't you?" Jeannie demanded.

Tight-lipped Nan said, "I've got to, for Lew, but for your sake, honey, I hope you never see Ed Lake again."

Jeannie began packing with desperate haste. She would see Ed, in Santa Fe. She would ask him why he had hidden the money and he'd tell her. There had to be an explanation, there had to be.

# Chapter Nine

**WORDEN** did not lock the door leading into the jail after Jeannie left. When McNamara came in with the tray, Worden opened the door for him and waited there until the deputy returned from Lake's cell.

Worden said, "Go get your supper, Mac," and shut the door.

McNamara didn't say anything until he locked the door and tossed the key ring to the desk where it struck with a ringing, metallic sound. He licked his lips, his eyes on Worden. "Jeannie have her last cry over Lake?" he asked.

Worden nodded. "Fetched him a cherry pie."

"You pick the cherries apart to see if she smuggled a gun to him?"

"I was going to," Worden said. "Had my knife out to cut the pie, then she started raising Cain about wanting Lake to see it that way and letting him cut it." Worden grinned a little. "Hell, Mac, she couldn't put a gun in a pie, so I took it back to Lake."

McNamara grabbed up the key ring and swung to the corridor door. He stopped, wavering as indecision gripped him, then tossed the key ring back on the desk. He said grumpily, "You're the boss."

"Maybe you picked the chicken and dumplings apart to see if the hotel clerk hid a gun for him."

"Nobody but Jeannie would do anything for that bastard," McNamara snapped, then realized Worden was joshing him. "All right, Bill. I'm so damned screwed up I'm about to pop. Main Street's dead enough to bury. I tell you I don't like it."

"You want the National Guard?" Worden asked.

"No. If we can't do the job, we'd better quit." He ran a hand through his red hair. "Fifteen hours to wait. Gonna seem like a year." He walked to the hall door. "I'll go get my supper."

Fifteen hours! No, a little less than that, for it was now after six. Worden filled his pipe and walked to the window. He stood there, watching lightning play across the sky and listened to the thunder. The storm was moving into the valley and would hit town in another hour or two.

For some reason which he did not fully understand, Jeannie was in his mind. He had always disliked her mother because of her domineering manner, but he liked Jeannie for the opposite reason.

As long as he could remember, Jeannie had been a shy, almost backward girl. She had not changed when she had become a woman; she had not changed visibly after her mother had died. Worden could understand that. A dove raised by a hawk does not become something else after the hawk is gone.

The rank injustice of the whole thing bothered Worden. Lake had ruined Jeannie as far as Gunlock was concerned. She had to get out of town. She would probably just walk out and leave her house and furniture and most of her clothes.

What was ahead for her? She had little or no money. Perhaps she could get a job somewhere if she could go far enough so her story would not follow her. But she'd read in the newspapers about Lake's hanging. If Worden judged her right, she would never love another man. She might not die of a broken heart, but she would be better off if she did.

And then, as it did so often these days, Worden's mind turned to Ellen and George Ballard. Ellen was not like Jeannie, but both were women, capable of loving in a way that was beyond a man's understanding. They translated all of reality in the light of that love. There was no logic about it; there was no use reasoning with them.

He pondered this, pulling steadily on his pipe, and the thought crowded into his mind again that maybe Ellen was not in love with George Ballard as much as she was in love with his money and position. She wouldn't realize it if it were true. She certainly wouldn't admit it if he asked her. Probably it wasn't true, just wishful thinking on his part.

His pipe went cold in his mouth and he relighted it. Maybe tomorrow when this was finished, he'd have a talk with Ada about Ellen and Ballard. It was useless for him to say anything to Ellen. There was this strange barrier between them. Besides, women measured men by different standards than men used. The characteristics which he recognized in Ballard and disliked would not bother Ellen.

It was a man's world as Jeannie's mother had said so often in her bellicose manner. A woman could scorn men and live her own life as Mrs. Mason had done. Or she could love a man and have her life ruined if she picked the wrong man as Jeannie had.

Worden thought of his wife. Ada was happy, he told himself. He was as sure of that as he could be sure of anything. Her life revolved around him and the children. He was a little awed when he considered how completely she had merged her will and desires with his.

Perhaps, and this was a new thought to him, a woman's love for a man was like a man's concept of duty. If it reached the point where he had to die because of Ed Lake, that's what he would do. Not because he wanted to die. He had no choice. It had been that way when first John Harris, then Judge Webb and Doc Quinn, had wanted him to wire the governor for help.

He had to do this job because it was his to do. McNamara, Worden was sure, felt the same. A man could be afraid. Any normal man was afraid under conditions like this, but still he did what he had to do. Nothing could change him. If Ellen did feel that way about Ballard, then no one, not even her father, had the right to ask her to give him up.

He heard someone in the hall, and swung around, a hand on the butt of his gun; then he saw it was John Harris, a Bible under his arm. Harris said, "I thought it was time I was coming. If Lake wants to talk, I may be with him a long time."

"We'll see," Worden said, and knocking his pipe into his hand, stuffed it into his pocket.

He unlocked the corridor door and pulled it open. Noticing that the light was thin back here in the jail, he fished a match out of his pocket and touched the flame to the wick of the lamp that hung from the ceiling.

Lake sat on his bunk, digging into the cherry pie that was on his lap. He grinned at Worden, a wicked, triumphant grin that seemed out of place on the lips of a man who had only a few hours to live.

"This is the first time I ever got filled up on cherry pie," Lake said. "Jeannie's a damned good cook." He motioned to the empty dishes on the tray. "That widow in the hotel ain't so bad, neither. This is better'n the swill you been fetching me, Sheriff."

"The Reverend is here to see you, Lake," Worden said.

Harris, the Bible in his hand, said, "I would like to pray with you and read the Book. You will be facing your Maker . . ."

128

"Damn you and your sniveling prayers," Lake shouted. "I ain't meeting my Maker as soon as you and Worden figure." He slammed the pie plate down on the bunk beside him and crossed to the cell door. "I'll tell you gents something you don't know. You ain't stretching my neck in the morning. Now get out of here."

"You are placing your faith on a thin reed," Harris said. "A man has no strength except that which is given him by God. There is still time to save your soul . . ."

"Shut off that hogwash," Lake jeered. "You're wrong, Preacher, plumb wrong. A man's strength comes from picking the right side. That's what I done. There's some folks in this county who don't want me to swing because they're afraid I'll talk, so they'll take care of me."

"The courts have turned your appeal down," Worden said, "and the governor has refused to act. You haven't got a chance . . ."

"You'll see what chance I've got." Lake wiped his mouth that was sticky with syrup from the pie. "Let me alone. My belly ain't full yet."

He stomped back to his cot and picked up the pie plate. Worden touched Harris' arm. "No use."

Harris nodded, and they walked back down the corridor. As Worden locked the door, he said, "I'm sorry."

"It was my duty to try," Harris said. "I don't understand him. He must know that nothing can save him unless . . ." He stopped, not wanting to say what was in his mind.

"Unless his friends break him out," Worden finished. "I expect them to try." He hesitated, then said, "Jeannie Mason brought that pie. She's leaving town tonight. I've been thinking about her. No matter what that ornery booger's done, she loves him."

"And you're sorry for her," Harris said.

"I am," Worden murmured.

Harris nodded. He pulled at his mustache, wanting to say something but not knowing how it would be received, then he said, "Come to church sometime, Sheriff. We need men, you know. When I look at my congregation on Sunday morning, I wonder why the greatest thing in all the world does not appeal to men. I feel as if my life has been a failure."

"No one else feels that way," Worden said, shocked by what the preacher had said. Then he thought he had reason to feel the same way. There would be no help from anyone except Orval Jones. He and McNamara stood alone. "I'll come to church. For the first time in my life, I'm beginning to realize that I'm not strong enough to do what has to be done."

"A man and God make a strong team," Harris said.

As Harris walked toward the door, Worden asked, "You'll be here in the morning?"

Harris glanced back, nodding. "I'll be here."

He went out, and Worden filled his pipe and

lit it. He paced restlessly around the room, watching the last of the daylight fade, his mind on Lake who felt too confident and defiant for a man in his position. Presently Orval Jones climbed the stairs and lit the hall lamp, then came on into the jail office.

"Why don't you light your lamp, Sheriff?" Jones asked. "Ain't out of coal oil, is it?"

"No," Worden answered. "I just like it dark, I guess."

"Beginning to rain." Jones lit the wall lamp. "Gonna be a hell of a storm, looks like." He hesitated, eyeing Worden, then blurted, "I don't aim to push myself, Sheriff, but you holler if you need help."

"Sure," Worden said. "I'll holler."

Jones left, and Worden began to pace again, the minutes dragging. It was nearly eight now, thirteen hours, and he wished he knew what Lake was counting on. There had been no mob violence in Grant County since Worden had taken the star.

He thought about Lew Hogan and Jess Ryman and Ballard's foreman, Jiggs Larribee. And Ballard who would not be with them if they came. If they did attack the jail, Ballard would be the one to give the word. But would he? Worden could not tell.

McNamara came in and, taking off his hat, slapped it against his leg. "Better hustle, Bill. It's gonna let go in about a minute. You'll be wet as a drowned rat just getting to the hotel."

Worden put on his Stetson. "Anybody in town yet?"

"Quiet as a tomb," McNamara said.

Outside it was completely dark except for the lighted windows along Main Street. A fine rain was in the air, actually more of a mist than a rain, but it was enough to make the boardwalk slippery, and Worden's feet almost went out from under him as he hurried toward the hotel.

A great clap of thunder rattled the windows just as he reached the lobby, then he heard the train whistle, a long, shrill sound that came to him sharply through the damp air. The eight o'clock eastbound was on time.

He crossed the lobby into the dining room, noting that Marv Tremaine was not behind the desk. No other customers were in the dining room. The waitress, Mary Barton, the storekeeper's girl, came to him at once. "You just got here in time, Sheriff," she said. "It's closing time."

"Steak," Worden said, and leaned against the back of the chair, slack-muscled and tired.

The rain struck then, coming down in sheets as if someone had upset a giant bucket over the town. He heard it beat against the windows, the panes black rectangles against the night darkness.

Mary brought his meal presently, saying, "Been working up to this for a long time. Be good for the grass, I guess."

"Yeah, I guess it will be," Worden said,

thinking that this was the kind of talk you heard from the townspeople. It would not occur to any of them that a rain would be good for the farmers' crops. At heart Gunlock was still a cow town.

Mary brought a bottle of ketchup from a nearby table. "How's your prisoner, Sheriff?"

Irritated, he said harshly, "Still there."

She went away, a little hurt by his tone. She didn't understand, he thought. But who did, except McNamara? He doused the steak with ketchup and began to eat, absently listening to the hard pound of the rain. He'd be wet before he reached the courthouse. Ada would scold him for not bringing his slicker.

He was starting on his pie when Marv Tremaine came into the lobby, stomping his feet and cursing the storm. He yanked off his slicker and threw it and his hat across a chair. He glanced into the dining room, and seeing Worden, came in and sat down across from him.

"I've been wanting to talk to you," Tremaine said. "Mary, fetch me a piece of pie and a cup of coffee. Man, this sure is a rain. Can't see three feet in front of you. Almost got lost coming from the depot."

"What were you doing at the depot?"

Tremaine didn't answer until Mary brought his pie and coffee and moved away, then he said in a low tone, "Just wanted to be sure Jeannie Mason got on the eight o'clock. That's what I wanted to see you about. I dunno if I done right or not. She came in this evening with a note from you asking me to give her Lake's valise. Looked damned funny to me. Nothing in his valise but some of his duds." He waggled his fork at Worden. "She paid up his room rent, you know. Done it before the trial, but what I want to know is why."

"I never figured it out." Worden spilled tobacco into the bowl of his pipe and lit it. "I sent the note, all right. It wasn't a forgery, if that's what's worrying you."

"Yeah, it was," Tremaine said, troubled. "But I still don't know why she wanted it."

"She didn't say," Worden said. "I guess I'm a little soft when it comes to Jeannie."

Tremaine leaned forward, scowling. "Damn it, Bill, you'd gone through his duds. Nothing she could use. She sure as hell wouldn't tote 'em with her."

"It's their business. Nobody got hurt by her taking the valise. We'd just have to throw it away," Worden pulled on his pipe, then added, "Anyhow, I'm glad she's gone."

Tremaine slammed an open palm against the table. "You still ain't told me why. I say it don't make sense."

"Just sentiment, I reckon." A flash of lightning threw vivid, twinkling flame against the windows, and the thunder followed a moment later. "Marv, you used to be a rancher. Speaking of things that don't make sense, you selling out to Ryman and buying this hotel always seemed crazy to me."

Tremaine's face turned red. "Had to have some kind of a business," he mumbled.

Tremaine was a short, stocky man who had run cattle north of Ryman's spread as long as Worden had been in the county, until about a year ago. In most ways he was a mild, easygoing man, but he had been a member of several of Worden's posses, and Worden knew that in a pinch he was a good man to have along.

"Might help if you'd tell me about it," Worden said.

So Tremaine told him, talking hesitantly, about the meeting at Ballard's house and why he had sold out. "But I dunno what happened after that. I just couldn't go along with the rest of them. Seemed like getting out was the only thing I could do."

"They sent for Lake," Worden said. "They must have."

Tremaine wiped a hand across his face. "Damn it, Bill, you're guessing."

Worden took the pipe out of his mouth and tamped the tobacco down. He was guessing, all right, and you don't hang a man because you have a guess, but it was plain logic that Lake had been brought here to commit the murders, and he'd been paid. But were all the cowmen equally guilty, or was it just the man who had written the letter to Lake?

"You know the talk that's going around," Worden said. "If the boys try to bust Lake out of jail, there'll be a hell of a fight, but they won't get him."

"Didn't figure they would," Tremaine said.

"I could use another deputy," Worden said.

Tremaine pushed his chair back. "I sold my ranch to keep out of trouble. I ain't sticking my nose into it now. I've got a wife and a kid."

"I've got a wife and two kids," Worden said.

"It's your job." Tremaine's face was red again. "Not mine."

"It's the job of every citizen to see that the law is enforced," Worden said angrily.

Tremaine rose. "Sorry, Bill. Running the hotel is my job."

Worden got up, too. He looked at Tremaine, but the man could not meet his gaze. Worden said, "I'm surprised, Marv. There's some I knew I couldn't count on, but I figured you were different."

"No different." Tremaine stared at the floor. "If I was hankering for a fight, I'd have kept my spread."

"You've ridden with me," Worden said. "You've got a man's share of guts. What's happened to you?"

Tremaine looked at him then. "They're my friends, Bill. I've known Jess Ryman for twenty years. Lew Hogan. Jiggs Larribee." He swallowed. "George Ballard. Hell, I couldn't shoot one of 'em. Not even for the law you worship."

Worden walked out. Tremaine called, "Take my slicker, Bill."

Worden put it on and slapped his hat on his head. George Ballard! Maybe he was the answer. Tremaine was afraid to stand against him. Ed Lake had known what he was doing. He had picked the right side.

Worden went out into the rain. It was then nine o'clock. Twelve hours to wait.

# *Chapter Ten*

**NAN** Hogan stood in the doorway of the Mason house, watching Jeannie hurry down the hill toward the depot. A fine rain was in the air, turning the top dust to mud. The storm would cut loose any minute. Nan hoped Jeannie reached the depot ahead of it. She would be on the train all night.

Then Jeannie disappeared in the thinning light. A flash of lightning gave Nan a last glimpse of Jeannie's slight figure, half running, the big suitcase banging at her legs. A strange girl, Nan thought moodily, child-like in so many ways, but a woman in her devotion to Ed Lake. Stupid, foolish, still clinging to her faith that he was not the man the law said he was simply because he had been kind to her.

Perhaps more than anyone else in Gunlock, Nan could understand how it was with Jeannie. But Nan still could not understand why Lake had picked Jeannie in the first place. How could a vicious and cruel man like Lake be capable of showing gentleness and kindness to Jeannie?

Nan heard the train whistle, still a mile from Gunlock, a long, poignant sound that awakened in her a nameless longing for distant places she would never see. It was one thing she missed, living so far from town.

Presently the storm struck with savage, sodden violence, a sheet of water that was like a silver curtain drawn across the town and hiding the lamplight in the windows of the closest house. Nan stepped back and closed the door, knowing that Jeannie had reached the depot before the deluge came. She closed the windows that had been open all day, her thoughts lingering on Jeannie.

She wondered what sort of life Jeannie would have in some distant place among strangers. Jeannie did not make friends easily. If Lake escaped, he'd go to her because she had the money. He'd take it and leave her, for that was the kind of man he was.

Nan looked around the room, remembering that the furniture was hers. Her gaze touched the little oak table with its slender, curved legs and brass claws at the base, each holding a glass ball, then went on to the walnut sideboard with the blue-flowered plates behind the glass doors, the leather rocking chair, the velvet love seat that had once been orange and was faded now to a dingy yellow.

A greedy hunger to possess all of this crowded into Nan, but she had room in the cabin for only a few extra pieces of furniture. She would have to decide what to take. She might have trouble with Lew about it. He'd say she had no right to any of it, that stuff like this wasn't practical, anyhow. It would be out of place among the pieces of rude, serviceable furniture they already had.

But he'd have to let her take some of it, she told herself fiercely. The blue-flowered plates. The pink, hobnail lamp with the green shade, the linen in the drawers of the sideboard. The food in the pantry. Lew would see some sense to that.

She picked up the lamp and went into Jeannie's bedroom. She set the lamp down on the marble-topped bureau and ran her fingers over the smooth surface. She had never owned anything like this in her life. It would crowd the leanto bedroom, but she'd find room for it.

She opened one of the top drawers. Handkerchiefs, smelling of lavender, a Bible, an ancient, dog-eared speller, an autograph book that probably dated back to Jeannie's years in grade school, a diary, and a few letters. These were the things Jeannie had not had room for in the suitcase, and they were the things she would miss the most, for they were links to her childhood.

Nan felt a little guilty, as if she were prying into Jeannie's privacy, but it would be far worse to leave them for George Ballard or someone else to find. She'd take them to the cabin, and then, if Jeannie never came back, she would destroy them.

She glanced through the letters, wondering if she should destroy them now. There was no sense in even thinking about Jeannie coming back. It didn't make any difference what happened to Lake in the morning. Jeannie couldn't come back. The Gunlock women had already decided that.

Nan would never forget how Jeannie had met her at the door, saying, "It's been a long time since anyone came to see me. I'm, well, maybe you don't know . . ." She had been filled with a pathetic longing to talk to another woman, but she had thought she should warn Nan. She had been starved by neglect, and that, Nan thought, must have strengthened her love for Ed Lake. He was the only one she had.

The bottom envelope was addressed to Lake. Nan stared at the words, each letter neatly printed in pencil. There was a single sheet inside. Nan took it from the envelope and smoothed it out. Just one sentence. "You'll be convicted, but you won't hang unless you try to implicate someone else."

No date. No name. Not even a signature. But Nan knew who had written it. She had gone to church occasionally with George Ballard when she was engaged to him. Not that church meant anything to him. Just good business to be seen there once in a while, he'd said. Besides, he made a sizable contribution every year and he might as well get a little entertainment for his money.

She usually sat behind Mrs. Mason because she had a broad back and consistently wore a tremendous cartwheel hat that hid Nan from the preacher's eyes. Ballard, with his perverse sense of humor, would take pencil and paper from his pocket and write cynical observations about the

141

people around them, like Tad Barton who sang in the choir so he could show off his tenor voice.

Nan would almost choke with laughter. Once she had to get up and walk out. Ballard had written, "Mrs. Mason, they tell me, refers to God as She." Nan remembered giggling about it for weeks. It was so typical of Jeannie's mother. And Ballard had printed every letter, neatly and precisely just as this note to Lake was written.

Nan picked up the lamp and hurried into the kitchen. She remembered the sheet of paper that Lake had kept under the false bottom of his suitcase with the money. She had been so excited about the money she hadn't even picked the paper up.

Nan found it on the floor where Jeannie had left it. She kicked the suitcase and Lake's clothes under the table, picked up the paper and flattened it out. It was the letter that had brought Lake to Grant County in the first place, every word printed as Ballard had once printed his smart little observations about the people in church.

Nan sat down and laid the two notes side by side. She had no idea how Jeannie had obtained the one that had been in the bureau drawer unless she had been given Lake's mail at the post office. But there was no puzzle about the other one. Ballard had sent it to Lake who had kept it, perhaps thinking he could blackmail the writer for more money at some later time.

When Ballard had talked to Nan that morning,

she had been sure he was responsible for the murders, not Lew. But she'd had no proof then and she didn't now. These notes satisfied her, but they wouldn't satisfy a jury, and Bill Worden would tell her that if she took them to him.

She sat there a long time, a savage bitterness gripping her. Of all the people in Grant County, she was the one who would not be believed if she accused Ballard of bringing Lake to Grant County. Sure, people would say skeptically, Ballard had jilted her and now she was trying to get even.

Ballard, with the agile maneuvering of a sand lizard, had worked it so Jeannie and Nan, or Lew as he thought, were doing a nasty job to save his neck. He wanted only one thing, to keep Lake from talking.

Nan got up and walked around the kitchen, hating Ballard as she had never hated him before, not even when he'd told her he was done with her. A dirty, slimy man, she thought wildly, protecting his place on Gunlock's pedestal. Now, knowing all that she did, she was still helpless. If she didn't get Lake out of jail, Lew would try, and he'd be killed, or sent to prison.

Lake must know who had sent for him. He might name Ballard before he hanged, but that didn't change anything for her. She wasn't worried about Lake naming Lew as Ballard had suggested he might. It was what Lew planned to do tonight that terrified her.

There was no use finding Lew and trying to

reason with him. He had a stubborn streak, and she had learned on several occasions that once his mind was made up about something he considered important, he'd go ahead.

She glanced at the alarm clock on a shelf behind the stove. Almost ten! She had no idea where the time had gone. She opened the back door and looked out. The rain had stopped. She closed the door, carried the lamp into the front room, and picking up the gun from the couch where she had left it, blew out the lamp and left the house.

She shivered as she went down the hill. She kept to the sidewalk, but it was black dark, and when she had to cross the street, the mud was ankle deep. Suppose Worden caught her? The thought brought a pressure to her chest that made it hard to breathe. It was the first time in her life she had ever done anything which, by her own standards, was completely wrong. And this was. If Lake escaped and killed another man, the killing would be upon her soul.

But she went on, keeping to a side street until she reached the courthouse square. She wondered if Lew, planning with Ryman and the others on how to break Lake out of jail, was having the same thought she was.

She paused under a tall poplar and studied the courthouse. The only light in the building that was visible to her was in a second-story window. That would be the jail office, she thought. Probably McNamara was there. Or Worden.

144

She crossed the lawn, moving rapidly. The lightning had stopped, but the sky was still overcast. It seemed to her she had never been out in a night as black as this one. She could not see anyone, could not hear anything, just the whisper of the leaves that was barely audible to her.

When she was directly below the lighted window, she edged along the courthouse wall until she thought she was under the window of Lake's cell. There was no way to be sure. Then, as she stood there staring upward, she realized for the first time that the whole thing was a crazy idea. In this darkness she could not see the string that Lake had let down from his window.

She eased along the wall to the corner and back, her arm extended, hoping her fingers would touch the cord, but she felt nothing except the rough bricks of the wall. For a moment panic crowded through her. There had to be some way to get the gun to Lake, there had to be. Maybe she could go upstairs and get permission to visit Lake. But then they'd know she was the one, and she shrank from that. It wouldn't work anyhow. They'd search her and find the gun.

She leaned against the wall, breathing hard as she tried to think of something she could do, then she heard the faint click of metal on the bricks of the courthouse wall. It came again and then again in a regular rhythm of timing. Not far from where she stood.

She moved toward the sound, realizing it was above her. She reached up and found the string, a knife tied to the end of it. Funny she hadn't thought of that, weighting the end so the wind wouldn't catch it.

She untied the knife with awkward, trembling fingers and dropped it to the ground. She ran the string through the trigger guard of the gun and knotted it securely, gave the string two quick tugs, and let go. She heard the gun scraping against the wall as Lake pulled it up. She waited until the sound died, then she ran back across the lawn to the poplars and stopping, leaned against one of them, breathing hard.

For a time it seemed she could not move. She expected to hear gun shots, but none came. She was no better than George Ballard, she thought dully. Or Jeannie. Or Lew. No, she was worse than Lew who wouldn't think of a sneaky thing like this. He'd go into the courthouse with his gun in his hand and later the law could do what it would with him.

She started back up the hill to Jeannie's place. She had put her horse in the barn behind the house. Now she'd find a lantern and saddle up and leave town. She had done what she had bargained to do.

But when she reached Jeannie's house, she knew she could not leave town. She'd stay for an hour or two, then go back and find out what happened. The town that now seemed deserted would be stirred to life and there would be no trouble finding out how it had gone. Probably Worden would be getting a posse together.

She went into the house and felt her way through the front room and on across the kitchen. It took a moment of fumbling to locate the box of matches on the warming oven. She took a handful, struck one, and went back to the front room and lighted the hobnail lamp.

She stumbled to the love seat and dropped down on it, her damp clothes clinging to her. It hadn't been raining when she was out. She was sweating, and now, thoroughly chilled, she began to shake.

In that moment she hated herself for listening to Ballard and for taking his money. She should have thrown it in his face and walked out. She'd bring it to town the first time she came and give it back.

Ellen Worden could have him and welcome to him. She didn't know Ellen very well, or her mother. Nice, respectable women, the kind who would make it impossible for Jeannie Mason to ever come back to Gunlock.

The thought occurred to her that Ellen didn't deserve marriage to George Ballard. She should go to Ellen and warn her. She laughed hysterically. Ellen would thank her for that.

Lake should be on his way by now. She had left the front door open, but with this wind blowing, she was probably too far from the courthouse to hear gunshots. There were five loads in the gun. Enough to kill McNamara and

Worden! She sat upright. She hadn't thought of that. She had considered only the other possibility, that Lake might be killed. But she had no assurance it would work that way.

Then the bitter agony of regret was in her. She thought: *Not even Lew is worth Worden's or McNamara's life.*

# *Chapter Eleven*

**A** few minutes after ten Worden, sitting at his desk in his office, heard someone on the stairs. A loose board squeaked under a man's weight. Worden had ordered Orval Jones to leave it loose, for it was a perfect warning signal. As McNamara had said, a mouse couldn't reach the second floor without telegraphing his approach.

Worden eased out of his chair, and picking up the double-barreled shotgun he had brought from the jail, moved to the door and waited there, both hammers back. Then Marv Tremaine came into view. He looked at the shotgun, gave Worden a weak grin, and said, "I surrender, Sheriff."

Worden swore, and lowering the muzzle of the shotgun, eased down the hammers. "I didn't figure it was you, Marv," he said. "Come in."

Worden went back to his desk and laid the shotgun across it. Tremaine came in, a little uneasy. He was remembering what had been said in the hotel dining room earlier that evening, Worden thought, and regretting it, had come to offer his help.

But it wasn't exactly that way. Tremaine stood in the middle of the room, his hands jammed into his pants' pockets. He said, "Bill, you've been sticking pretty close to the courthouse the last few days, so I don't reckon you've heard the talk. But I hear plenty in the hotel, or in the Casino. I usually drop in for a drink or two every evening."

Worden said, "Well?"

Tremaine cleared his throat. "The first trouble you have will come from the farmers. I just took a sashay down past the church. They're inside, just about every man and boy who lives south of the creek. They don't aim to wait till nine o'clock in the morning to see Lake hang."

So Marv Tremaine didn't think he'd heard the talk. Hell, it was all he had heard lately. This was the third time today. First from John Harris, then from Doc Quinn and Judge Webb, and now from Tremaine.

Worden wasn't sure why Tremaine was telling him this, so he said again, "Well?"

"I thought you ought to go to the meeting before anything starts," Tremaine blurted. "I was a cowman too long to cotton to sodbusters, but I've found out these boys ain't so bad at that. They come into the hotel for a meal, and once in awhile I take a drink with 'em in the Casino. You got a lot of votes from them the last time you ran, so I figure if you went down and talked to them, they might listen."

"And they might take a notion to hang me along with Lake," Worden murmured. "Want to go with me, Marv?"

Tremaine's eyes were suddenly defiant. "I

150

ain't no hero. I told you that a while ago."

"Neither am I," Worden said. "How about it?"

Tremaine sighed. "All right. I'll go. I won't do no good, but I'll go."

"I was banking on that. Wait till I tell Mac."

Worden put on his hat, walked down the hall to the jail, and told McNamara where he was going. When he returned, Tremaine was standing at the head of the stairs. It occurred to Worden that this might be a trap, that Tremaine had been talked into luring him away from the courthouse so McNamara would be alone.

He walked along the hall and down the stairs, uncertain about this. Then he decided he was being too suspicious. Tremaine wasn't that kind. Besides, he had removed himself from the cowmen when he'd sold out to Jess Ryman and bought the hotel. Tremaine was probably the last man in Grant County they'd go to for help.

But caution was again a controlling force in Worden. When they reached the bottom of the stairs, he told Tremaine to wait, and going into the basement, asked Orval Jones to stay with McNamara while he was gone.

"Glad to, Sheriff, glad to," Jones said, and ran into his living quarters for his guns.

McNamara would welcome Jones' company, Worden thought as he joined Tremaine. He grinned when he stepped outside. He'd hear from Mac when he got back.

It was very dark, heavy clouds covering the sky

151

so that the starlight could not break through. The storm was over, although lightning still played above Red Mountain, and thunder was a distant sound.

The air remained damp and cold, but the chances were good the clouds would break away before dawn. Worden hoped they would. Darkness like this would cover the cattlemen if they attacked the courthouse, but even starlight, thin as it would be, might prove a deterrent to them.

When they reached the Casino, Tremaine gripped Worden's arm. He said, "Jess is here."

Lamplight coming through the windows and above and below the batwings made yellow stains on the wet sidewalk and muddy street. There was no mistaking Jess Ryman's sorrel that was racked in front of the saloon. Worden looked through a window. Ryman was at the bar talking to the apron.

"I'm going in," Worden said. "Stay outside if you don't want to side me."

"Might as well tag along," Tremaine grunted, and followed Worden into the Casino.

Ryman spun around, and when he saw who had come in, his weather-wrinkled face had the guilty look of a kid caught with his hand in the cookie jar. He wrapped his right hand around his gun butt, calling, "I ain't done nothing, Sheriff."

Worden moved directly toward the rancher, sensing the panic that was in him. It was touchy,

Ryman being the hot-tempered man he was. Worden said, "But you're fixing to do something, aren't you, Jess?"

"Just rode to town for a drink," Ryman said defensively. "No crime in that."

Worden saw that Tremaine had moved to the center of the room so that he faced Ryman's side. Worden stopped two paces in front of Ryman, not sure about Leo Roos, the bartender. Roos made no secret of the fact that his sympathies were with the cowmen. The bulk of his business came from them, particularly Ballard's Lazy B hands, but Worden didn't think he had the guts to back Ryman if it came to a showdown.

"Jess," Worden said, "from the looks of your clothes, you got caught in the rain. Late as it is, with the storm and all, I don't believe you rode in just for a drink."

"Wasn't raining when I left home," Ryman said sullenly.

"Why did you say you hadn't done anything if you hadn't?" Worden asked.

Ryman threw a glance at Roos to see if he would have any backing, but apparently he had no encouragement from the barman. He backed away, licking dry lips as he looked at Tremaine. He said, "So you're sucking around after the law, are you, Marv? Figger you got me hipped, don't you?"

"Looks like it," Tremaine said.

"An innocent man doesn't act as guilty as you do," Worden said. "Why did you come to town?

153

Aiming to meet the rest of the boys here, maybe?"

"I came to town for a drink, damn it," Ryman shouted. "You got no cause to hooraw me."

Worden took another step toward him. "If you hadn't started yapping about not having done anything, me and Marv would have had a drink and pulled out. But you had to tell me how innocent you are. So I figure you're up to something, and I want to know what it is."

Ryman backed up another step. "Stay away from me, Worden. You ain't gonna run over me just because you're toting a star."

"I've heard talk that you boys aim to bust Lake out of jail," Worden said. "I'll run over anybody who tries it and don't you forget it."

He took two long strides toward Ryman. The rancher, giving way to his panic, started to pull his gun. Tremaine cried, "Hold it, Jess." Ryman, thinking he was covered, stopped his draw, the gun barely out of leather.

Worden, close now, batted the gun barrel to one side with his left hand and cracked Ryman in the face with his right fist. Roos shouted, "No call for that, Sheriff."

Ryman, spun around by the blow, grabbed the bar and held himself upright as Worden jerked the gun out of his hand. Ryman, hurt and angry, cried out, "You'll never get elected again, Worden. You're too damned smart for your britches."

"You're going to jail," Worden said.

Roos swore. "You got nothing against him. What the hell did he . . ."

He stopped when Worden looked at him. "He pulled a gun on a lawman, Leo. That'll do to hold him." He shoved Ryman's revolver under his waistband and drew his own. "Start walking, Jess."

Ryman shouted, "Tell the boys what happened, Leo. They'll tear that God-damned courthouse apart. You'll find out how big you are before morning, Worden."

"Move," Worden said.

Cursing, Ryman started toward the batwings. Worden said, "That's enough, Jess," and Ryman was silent.

They went along the boardwalk to the courthouse and up the stairs to the jail. McNamara ran into the hall when he heard the squeak of the loose board, a Winchester in his hands. He stopped when he saw who it was, then grinned when he glanced at Ryman's stormy face. "Another guest, Bill?" he asked.

"Yeah," Worden said. "Roll out the red carpet."

"Want me to get a chicken dinner for him?"

"Not till we decide we're going to hang him," Worden said.

Ryman wheeled, his face rigid with fear. He was a banty of a man, always edgy, and Worden knew that on every roundup he started more fights than any other three men. The fact that he never won didn't stop him the next time he lost

155

his temper. But now he knew he was into something big, and it was enough to make him lose his nerve.

"You can't hang a man because he pulls a gun on you," Ryman cried shrilly.

"Might change my mind if I knew why you were in town," Worden said.

Ryman shook his head, breathing hard. "Lock him up, Mac," Worden ordered, and waited while McNamara unlocked the door leading into the corridor and gave Ryman a shove. The little man went along, silent now, and when McNamara returned, Worden told him what had happened.

"Must have fetched a message of some kind," McNamara said thoughtfully, "but why did he go to Leo?"

"I wish I knew," Worden said. "Where's Orval?"

McNamara gave him a tight grin. "I chased him downstairs. Hell, all he wanted to do was talk. I couldn't stand it."

Worden sighed. He couldn't blame McNamara. "I'll be back as soon as I can," he said, and left the room.

Jones was waiting in the downstairs hall, so angry he was almost incoherent. "Who's running this shebang," he demanded, "you or that tough deputy of yours?"

"Sorry, Orval," Worden said. "Mac figures he can handle things. Guess I stepped on his pride."

He hurried out of the courthouse, not wanting to hear anything else from Jones. Everybody was edgy, he thought irritably. He had enough to worry about without salving Jones' injured feelings.

When he got back to the Casino, he saw that Leo Roos was sullen and Tremaine triumphant. Worden said, "Well?"

"I got it out of him," Tremaine said. "A man gets a pretty stiff sentence for obstructing justice, don't he, Sheriff?"

"Yeah," Worden agreed. "Real stiff."

"That's what I was telling Leo. Might be ten years, helping Ryman's bunch get Lake out." Tremaine nodded at the bartender. "Tell him, Leo."

"Jess came in to ask me to keep the Casino open after midnight," Roos said, still sullen. "I dunno what they're figgering on, but they'll be here before sunup." He poured himself a drink, his hand trembling, and added spitefully, "You'll have a hell of a scrap on your hands, Sheriff. Maybe you'll find out you're just one man."

"I've known that for quite awhile," Worden said. "Come on, Marv." When they were outside, he added, "I sure don't savvy this. Looks like they'd just ride in when they figure the sign's right."

"There's something else," Tremaine said. "Jess had just started to tell him. Something they wanted to find out before they tackled the jail."

Worden considered that as they walked toward the church. What else could there be except the farmers? The natural move for the cowmen to make would be to tackle the jail before the farmers did.

A sense of frustration added to the tension in Worden as this vague "something else" eluded him. He tried to put it out of his mind. Probably nothing to it. There was only one way to get Lake out of jail.

The church windows were lighted, and Worden could hear the singing just as he had that afternoon, but it was different, the bass and tenor of a crowd of men instead of the soprano and alto of women. He recognized the song, "Little Brown Church in the Vale." He had sung it as a boy in Iowa.

He took off his hat and went in, Tremaine a step behind him. Tremaine closed the door and the two of them stood together, Worden's gaze on Preacher Rigdon who was beating time to the music. They reached the final chorus, and Worden's mind spun back across the years, boyhood memories crowded into his thoughts as the familiar words came to him.

"Oh, come to the church in the wildwood,
Oh, come to the church in the dale,
No spot is so dear to my childhood
As the little brown church in the vale."

It wasn't the same as it had been this afternoon, not at all. There were forty or more men and boys in the room, their rifles and shotguns leaning against the wall. A young farmer was playing the organ, his blunt fingers possessing far less skill than the girl had demonstrated this afternoon. And somehow Rigdon had a different look about him, wild and triumphant as if he was close now to the moment he had been waiting for.

Tremaine nudged Worden with an elbow as Rigdon shouted, "Once more through the chorus, men." The bass "Come, come, come," seemed to go on and on, and Worden heard Tremaine whisper, "Go up front. Rigdon's seen us, but he'll act like he don't if you stay here."

Worden walked slowly up the aisle as the chorus came to an end, the echoes dying. Men turned and looked at him, surprise showing on their faces, then shock, and he realized Rigdon was furious. *He's like a mad dog*, Worden thought. *He's got the smell of blood in his nose.*

"You are desecrating the house of the Lord," Rigdon thundered. "Go away."

Worden looked up at him. He said, "I want to talk to these men." He turned and faced them, and it was then that he saw Ben Smith, the father of the murdered boy, sitting on the front seat, his surviving sons beside him.

"You are spawned by the devil," Rigdon shouted, "you and your future son-in-law. There is nothing for you to say."

"Is it wrong for the spawn of the devil to come

to church?" Worden asked.

Smith stood up. "Let him speak, Parson. He's right. There is no better place for him than in church."

A dozen men shouted, "Amen."

Rigdon swallowed, his Adam's apple bobbing up and down in his great neck. He said, "All right, have your say and go."

Worden was silent for a moment as he looked at the men who faced him. All ages, all sizes, all colors of eyes and hair, and yet somehow they looked alike, branded by the sun and wind and the hard work they had put into the unyielding land they plowed and sowed.

Good men at any other time, but now they had been worked up to the point where they were capable of murder. A sense of predestined failure beat at Worden's mind. Their faces were set and hard, their decision already made.

"Let me say first that I represent the law," Worden said. "I suppose the law means different things to different men. It isn't always honest, and it isn't always enforced, but ask yourselves whether either of these is true in Grant County, or ever has been since you came here."

This had been building for a long time, and in the hours they had been here together, Rigdon had come close to hypnotizing them. But they were listening to Worden, and he hurried on, "It seems strange to see guns in the house of the Lord. When I was a schoolboy, I remember reading in a history book about the Pilgrims bringing their guns to church to protect them from Indians, but there are no Indians in Grant County."

"All right, you've had your say," Rigdon shouted. "We will see that justice is done. You can't stop us with talk."

Smith, still standing, said, "He ain't finished, Parson."

Rigdon had lost ground and he must have sensed it. He said grudgingly, "Go on, Worden."

"I've heard what you intend to do," Worden said. "When I saw your guns, I knew that what I'd heard was true. Let me remind you that you will not take Lake from the courthouse without killing me and Mike McNamara, and that will make murderers out of you. You've all been in the courthouse. You know the stairs are narrow. Two men standing at the top will kill many of you. Your families need you, everyone of you."

"The Lord is on our side," Rigdon shouted. "His strength will be with us."

But his words fell upon fallow ground. Worden felt a sudden new hope when he saw that these men were thinking about what he had said. He went on, "There has been some dirty gossip about George Ballard being a stockman and wanting Lake out of jail, and because he is engaged to marry my daughter, it has been said that I'll let Lake go. It's a lie. If Ballard tries anything, I'll shoot him the same as I would any other man."

"He has to say that." Rigdon pounded his

pulpit. "But I tell you that if justice is done, it will be done by us."

"Lake was brought in by me and Mike McNamara," Worden said. "He was tried and convicted and sentenced to hang at nine o'clock tomorrow morning. I promise you it will be done. But any act of violence on your part will put you outside the law, and you would be punished for doing something that would be done legally a few hours later. Most of you voted for me. You must have trusted me or I would not have been elected. I'm asking only one thing. Trust me now."

Worden motioned toward Ben Smith who was still on his feet. "I know how you feel. It is right and proper that Ed Lake pay for what he did, but is there any justice in throwing away a dozen other lives for nothing?"

"No," Smith said as if he had not thought of it quite that way before. "There's no justice in that at all."

Rigdon placed both hands on the pulpit, palms down. He said, "We talk of justice. Is there any justice in letting the men who paid Lake for murder go free?"

This was the question Worden feared, the question for which he had no answer. He said, "If and when I have evidence against that man, or men, they will be arrested and tried, but it has nothing to do with what you propose to do. Let Ed Lake die at the time and in the way the law has said he should die."

Worden could say no more; he could do no more. He saw doubt and uncertainty in the faces of these men before him, even in the face of Ben Smith who should, of all of them, feel the greatest sense of injury. Worden walked down the aisle and left the church, Tremaine going out behind him.

As they strode along the boardwalk, Tremaine said, "You done it right, Sheriff. They hadn't done no thinking, but they sure as hell will now."

Worden sighed. "I don't know, Marv. I hope so."

"There's something wrong with Rigdon," Tremaine said. "He wants to pull the rope on Lake."

"Yeah, I know," Worden said, "but I'm not sure his people know it."

When they reached the hotel, Tremaine said, "Well, you done all you could."

"I guess I did," Worden said. "Thanks, Marv."

He went on, walking slowly and having no certainty in his mind that he had stopped this thing. But they would do some thinking as Tremaine had said, and it might be enough. He could not understand it. Once he had heard Judge Webb say that the seed of self-destruction was in every man. At the time it had seemed stupid, but it didn't now.

One side wanted to save Lake's life when it should not be saved. The other side wanted to take it before the law did. There was not the slightest bit of sense in either, and to cap it all, they were good, law-abiding men if taken individually.

He turned off the street toward the court-house, a pile of wood and brick that stood tall and black against the lesser blackness of the night. Then he caught a hint of movement somewhere in the deep darkness ahead of him, and he lunged off the boardwalk toward a poplar tree, his right hand pulling his gun as he moved.

# Chapter Twelve

**FOR** a long moment Worden stood there beside the trunk of the poplar, his gun in his hand, trying to see into the darkness. He had moved with the speed and instinct of a cat, fear running down his spine in sharp, muscle-tightening prickles.

He did not know who was there, but he supposed it was Lew Hogan or one of the other cowmen, waiting to shoot him. He had no illusions about his position. He was the target, the key man, and if he was killed, only Mike McNamara would stand between Ed Lake and freedom.

"Is that you, Mr. Worden?"

Relief was a weakness in his belly, a strange emptiness that hurt and made him incapable of answering for a moment. It was a woman who had called, a vaguely familiar voice that he could not identify for a moment. He slipped his gun back into its holster, then he was able to say, "I'm Worden."

It might be a trap, and he was immediately ashamed of the thought. The tension of these past days, particularly the last few hours, had brought a state of fear to him that he had never known before in his life. But this was a new situation for him, and he salvaged some pride from the knowledge that no man liked to be a sitting duck.

The woman was coming toward him; he heard the pound of boot heels on the wet boards of the walk, and because she could not distinguish him from the poplar trunk, she called, "Where are you, Sheriff?"

He recognized her voice then; it was Nan Hogan. Again he felt the sudden, savage thrust of fear. Of all the cowmen in Grant County, Lew Hogan was the one most likely to make trouble, and Nan was Lew's wife. Probably Lew was hiding somewhere in the shadows, his back pressed against the courthouse wall. He would open up as soon as Nan tolled Worden into the open.

She was not more than twenty feet from him when she stopped, and he could hear her ragged breathing. He drew his gun again, then she said, "I'm alone, Mr. Worden. I've got to talk to you. I've got to warn you."

"Against what?" he asked, still not moving.

"Lake has a gun. I tied it to a string and he pulled it up through his window. I don't think he's escaped yet, but he's had plenty of time. I was afraid you'd run into him. I just got here when I heard you coming."

She was working him for something, all right. No woman in her right mind would admit she had given Lake the means of escape. Besides, Lake didn't have any string. Even if he did, this kind of trickery wasn't Hogan's way. Or Nan's either.

She had located him. Now she came toward him, still breathing hard. He said, "I have my gun in my hand. If Lew tries anything, I'll kill him."

She stood within three feet of him, close enough for her dumpy figure to assume definite shape to his eyes. Her hands were at her sides. He couldn't tell if she had a gun, but he knew her well, well enough to gamble that she would not kill him for a man like Ed Lake.

"Lew isn't with me, Mr. Worden," Nan cried. "Please believe me. I've been terribly afraid that Lew would get into trouble because he thinks he has to get Lake out of jail. I thought that if I helped Lake get away, Lew wouldn't do anything. I didn't realize until it was too late that Lake might shoot you or McNamara. That's why I came back to warn you."

"You're lying," Worden said harshly. "You're teamed up with Lew. I know you're lying because Lake didn't have any string."

"I'm not lying," she said wearily. "Jeannie brought the string to Lake in the pie."

She could have, he thought with bitter self-condemnation. He remembered he had intended cutting the pie and Jeannie had given him the song and dance about it being the last thing she could bring Lake and she wanted him to cut it himself. He'd been easy because he'd felt sorry for Jeannie. He, Bill Worden, the tough lawman that most people thought didn't have a spoonful of sentiment in his makeup.

"How do you know Lake's still in jail?" he asked.

"I don't know. It's just that I hadn't heard any shooting. He might have tricked McNamara. Then if he found out you weren't in the building, he might be waiting inside to get you. You're the man he's afraid of. There's nobody else in the county who could run him down and he knows it."

She sounded as if she was telling the truth, and her guess about Lake waiting for his return made sense. Still, it seemed queer for her to go to all that trouble helping Lake escape, and then turn against him.

"I don't savvy," Worden said. "Helping Lake could send you to prison. Chances are I'd never have found out you were the one if you hadn't told me."

"It's up to you about me going to jail," she said dully, "but at least I won't be responsible for your death. Mr. Worden, I suppose that what a woman does often seems crazy to a man, but I love Lew. I was just trying to keep him out of trouble. That's why I did it, whether it makes any sense to you or not."

It did make sense, of a sort. She'd lost her nerve after she'd done it. He said, "Lew will still be in trouble if he tries to break Lake out of jail."

"I know," she said, "but your life or McNamara's isn't worth keeping Lew out of a

168

mess if he's bound to get into it. I've done all I can, but you stand here wasting time."

"We'll see," Worden said.

He still wasn't sure, but she was right about him wasting time. If he dawdled around and let McNamara get shot, or let Lake get away in the darkness, he'd be the laughing stock of Grant County. Of the whole country, for that matter, by the time the reporters got done with it.

He moved away from the tree, and keeping on the grass so he wouldn't be heard, started toward the courthouse door. Nan fell in beside him. She said, "I've got something to show you, Mr. Worden. You'll want to see it, since Ellen is your daughter."

At the moment her words made no sense to him. He walked slowly, the hammer of his gun pronged back, every sense alert. He still was not entirely sure this wasn't a trap. If Lew Hogan shot him, McNamara would come rushing out of the courthouse and he'd be killed. There would be no one to keep Hogan from freeing Lake, no one but Orval Jones.

He moved fast when he reached the steps leading to the courthouse door; he grabbed the knob and turned it and yanked the door open. Then he stopped, shocked by what he saw. Lake stood with his face to the wall, his hands over his head. Orval Jones was holding him there, his double-barreled shotgun in his hands.

Jones let out a squall when he saw Worden, a sound that was weighted with both relief and fear. He had long dreamed of being a hero, but Worden had never been sure he could be counted on when the blue chips were down. Yet here he was, holding a man who would have killed him without batting an eye if he had a chance.

"I never was so glad to see anybody in my life," Jones said, his voice high with excitement. "You can sure have him."

Jones lowered his shotgun and stepping back, leaned against the wall on the opposite side of the hall from Lake, so slack-bodied that he would have fallen if he hadn't braced himself.

Lake looked around. "By God, I'm glad to see you, too, Worden. I thought that fool was gonna blow my head off."

"Did you kill McNamara?" Worden asked.

"Hell no. He's in my cell."

A short-barreled revolver lay on the floor at Lake's feet. Worden asked, "How'd you get him, Orval?"

"I was damned sore, Mac kicking me out of his office like he done," Jones said, his voice still high. "I figured I'd keep watch down here, just in case something went wrong, and I'd show your smart alec deputy he wasn't so smart. Well, I heard that loose step squeak, and from the way Lake was easing along, I allowed it was him, so I waited around the corner till he got almost to the door. He was still moving slow and careful, and he didn't know I was behind him till I rammed my Greener into his back."

"You did a good job, Orval," Worden said. "All right, Lake. Back upstairs."

"I want to see Mac's face," Jones crowed. "I just want to see his face."

Without a word Lake climbed the stairs. He didn't even have the energy to curse Worden who had picked up his revolver and followed him. When they reached the jail office, Worden saw that the key ring was on the desk. He picked it up, saying, "Orval, pull the door open."

"Yes sir," Jones said, and tugged the heavy corridor door open.

McNamara, locked inside Lake's cell, began to shout. "We're coming," Worden yelled. "Shut up."

When Lake walked into the corridor, Jess Ryman got off his bunk and came to the bars. "What's the matter, Lake? I thought you'd be headed to Colorado before this."

Lake said nothing. Neither did McNamara as Jones unlocked the cell door and pulled it open. McNamara stepped out and Lake went in and Jones locked the door. Ryman said with satisfaction, "That bastard didn't have time to let me out of here. No sir, he was on his way. Why me and the boys ever lost any sleep over him I don't know."

"Maybe you'd like to tell them that," Worden said.

"Maybe I would," Ryman snapped, "if I was a free man, which I ain't."

"I'll see what I can do," Worden said, and went back to the office. "Well, Mac?"

"Yeah, speak up," Jones jeered. "How'd he . . ."

"Shut up, Orval," Worden said.

McNamara aimed a vicious kick at the desk and swore. "Rub it in, both of you. Go ahead and rub it in."

"I'm the one that got him, Bill," Jones said. "Me, Orval Jones. I'd make a better deputy than this red-headed galoot, but no . . ."

"Orval, you'll shut your mouth, and keep it shut, or you'll go downstairs and stay there." Worden nodded at McNamara. "What happened?"

"He got to raising Cain," McNamara said. "Yelling his head off for a doctor. I went back to see what was biting him, and he said you'd beaten hell out of Ryman. Claimed Jess was dying. I took a look at him. He was flat on his bunk like he was unconscious, and he didn't say anything when I asked him how he was. I got the keys, figuring I'd better take a good look before I sent Orval for Doc Quinn. Well, when I went back, Lake showed me that gun and told me to unlock his cell. I don't know how he got that gun, Bill, so help me I don't."

"I do," Worden said, and told him.

"So you should have cut that pie," McNamara said. "What do you know about that?"

"Now you can rub it in," Worden said. "Orval, if you let this out, I'll skin you. Savvy? I'll make a

172

purse out of your hide and throw the rest out to dry."

"Sure, sure," Jones said hastily. "I won't say a word."

"Like hell," McNamara grunted. "Well, he made me go into his cell and locked me in there. I thought he was going to drill me, but I guess he didn't want to risk a shot, knowing it'd fetch you."

"Orval, you'd best stay here with Mac," Worden said. "You'll enjoy his company, won't you, Mac?"

"Yeah," McNamara said sourly. "He can tell me stories."

Worden glanced at his watch. It was after eleven. Less than ten hours. He still did not know what the farmers would do, and Hogan and his bunch would make their try. When he left the room, he saw that Nan was waiting for him in the hall. He had completely forgotten about her.

"What were you going to show me, Nan?" he asked.

She handed him two folded pieces of paper. "George Ballard was the one who sent for Lake and paid him for the killings. Lake had a lot of money hidden in that valise. Jeannie got it."

Ballard, he thought, and knew suddenly what Nan had meant about Ellen. He went into his office and sat down at his desk, a sickness crawling into his belly. Nan followed him and dropped into a chair. Worden unfolded the sheets of paper and read the printed words, then looked up at Nan. She was very pale, a muscle in her right cheek beating with the regularity of a pulse.

He asked, "Where did you get these?"

"The one that brought him here was with the money," she answered. "You didn't find it because he had a false bottom in the valise. I found the other one in a drawer of Jeannie's bureau."

Worden shoved the letters away from him. "No signature, Nan. One man's printing looks like another."

She put her big hands on her thighs, fingers spread. She said, "Mr. Worden, this is hard for me to say because you know there was a time when I expected to marry George, but he wanted Ellen, not me, so I married Lew to save my pride. It was quite a while before I figured out George did me a good turn and that Lew was a better man than George would ever be. I told you I love him, but I suppose you're thinking I just want to get even with George."

Worden picked up his pipe and filled it. He had no doubt that Ballard was the man he wanted, that Ballard should hang alongside Ed Lake. But he couldn't take these letters into Judge Webb's court and get a conviction. Then he thought of Ellen and what it would do to her if she lost Ballard. But she would lose him, even if Worden had to resign his office and kill George Ballard.

"Go on," he said, and lighted his pipe.

She told him about Ballard's visit that morning, and added, "I decided to get that gun to Lake myself. I couldn't think of anything except to keep Lew out of it."

Worden laid the pipe down. He found no satisfaction in it; the smoke tasted bitter against his tongue. "Keep talking," he said.

"There's another thing," Nan said. "Jeannie didn't know about the money in the valise until Lake told her when she brought the pie, so she went to Ballard and got him to lend her five hundred dollars on her note. Do you think Ballard would have done that if he wasn't the one?"

Mechanically Worden picked up his pipe and drew on it. It had gone out and he laid it back on the desk. "No, but all we've got is circumstantial evidence that won't hold up in court."

"I suppose not," she said bitterly, "him being a Ballard, but a little man like Lew wouldn't have a chance." She leaned forward. "It would be legal evidence if you proved he owned the gun, wouldn't it?"

Worden took the revolver out of his pocket and laid it on the desk beside his pipe. "He wouldn't give you a gun that could be traced to him. Chances are he bought it somewhere else, maybe in Denver."

"Are you defending him?" she demanded. "Because of Ellen?"

He tilted back his chair and looked at the wall above Nan's head. He could not, even now, tell her he had disliked Ballard for a long time, that under no circumstances would he permit Ellen to marry him. It was not a thing he could talk about.

"No," he said, "but I'm an old hand at this business. I've seen more than one guilty man go free on evidence like this." He tapped the letters with his forefinger. "We can't prove someone else didn't write these. Might have been Lew."

"Lew has trouble spelling his own name," Nan said. "Look at those letters. An educated man wrote them." She paused, her eyes on Worden's face, then added, "George used to write notes to me. He printed every word, just like those letters to Lake."

Worden got up and walked around the room. The sickness had not left his belly, for it was impossible to keep from thinking about Ellen and what it would do to her if she lost Ballard. Or, on the other hand, what would happen if she married him, a man who was responsible for three murders.

"You stay here," he said. "I'm going to see George."

He strode out of the room. He wasn't sure what he would do. As he left the courthouse and started up the hill to Ballard's house, he wondered if he should resign tonight. He was thinking as a father now, not a lawman, and he was afraid of himself and what he might do, afraid he would disgrace the star he had worn with honor for so long.

# Chapter Thirteen

**WHEN** Ballard reached the house after leaving the Worden place, he told his housekeeper he would not be home for supper. That, after missing his noon meal, was too much. He fled from the kitchen, leaving the woman shouting at him in a shrewish voice. He went upstairs and took a bath, resolving that as soon as he got back from his honeymoon, he'd advertise for another housekeeper.

He changed to a brown broadcloth suit and patent leather shoes; he took more than usual care with his tie. In spite of the worry about Ed Lake that had been in the periphery of his consciousness for days, he was able to fasten his mind on his coming marriage. He had a great deal to offer a woman, he thought with satisfaction, far more than any other man in Gunlock, and he was sure Ellen was aware of it.

He combed his hair carefully, parting it on the right side and brushing the left side up and back so that it gave him the dignified appearance he sought. For a time he stood in front of the mirror, admiring himself. He and Ellen would make a fine looking couple, he thought. They'd stay in San Francisco for a month; he'd give her the run of the stores and she could buy all the clothes she wanted. With his advice, of course, for her choice was not always the best.

He'd take her to the opera. A boat ride in the bay. Anything she wanted. He might not even return to Gunlock. The Lazy B and the bank made a good living for him, and he could count on Jiggs Larribee's and Timothy Brown's loyalty and good judgment.

His day dreaming ended suddenly as he realized he was going to be late. He hastily packed a valise, a precaution more than anything else, for he had no way of determining how long he'd be at Worden's. But he thought he'd have plenty of time. Instead of taking the eight o'clock for Denver, they'd wait until midnight for the westbound. They'd be married in Salt Lake City and go on to San Francisco the next day.

It was after seven when he left his house. The storm was close now, and he hurried, not wanting to be caught out in it. Perhaps it wouldn't last long. If it did, he'd have to walk to the livery stable for his buggy and come back for Ellen. And he'd have to hire a man to drive the rig back to the stable. He should have made arrangements when he left the bank, but this whole thing had come into his mind suddenly and he hadn't planned ahead as he usually did.

Ellen answered his ring, and the instant he stepped into the hall, he sensed that something had gone wrong. She was wearing a blue silk dress he had not seen before, cut so that it hugged her firm, pointed breasts and slim waist.

It was probably a dress she had been saving for her honeymoon, and for some reason had decided to wear it tonight.

But it was her face that warned him. She was pale and she had been crying. There was no call for either. This should be her night of triumph. He held out his arms to her, but she turned as if she didn't see his gesture.

Opening the door into the parlor, she said in a low voice, "We're terribly late with supper, George. I hope you're not starving."

"I can wait." He followed her into the parlor, adding, "I like your dress, Ellen."

She glanced back, giving him a smile that seemed a little forced. "I'm glad, George. It's a special dress."

The fireplace was bright with flame, the crackle of the pitch pine a welcoming sound, but a perverse gust of wind had blown smoke into the room. It made a blue, writhing ribbon above the lamp on the table, and the air was heavy with the smell of it.

"Ellen."

She had started toward the dining room. Now she turned. "What is it, George?"

He came to her and took her hands. "Something's happened, Ellen. What is it?"

"Nothing. If you'll excuse me, I'll help Mamma. I'm sorry about the fireplace. Maybe it won't smoke any more."

She tried to tug free from his grip, but he wouldn't let her go. "Listen," he said. "We won't be able to make the eight o'clock, but there's a westbound train at midnight. We'll take it and get married in Salt Lake City and go on to San Francisco. You've never been there, have you?"

"No. Sit down, George. I've got to help Mamma."

He released her hands and watched her walk away. He drew a cigar from his pocket and lighted it, feeling let down. He had been sure Ellen would be wildly excited, but instead, she acted as if he had done something wrong.

He sat down in a black leather chair and glanced around the room with its meager furnishings. He knew what Bill Worden's salary was. Many men, probably most men, would have used their office to make something on the side, but not Bill Worden. Honesty was all right in principle, but a man was a fool to carry it to extremes.

Worden could use a few hundred dollars to furnish the house properly. The parlor, at least. This was the room people saw and they made their judgments from it. Mrs. Worden needed new clothes, too. She had one good taffeta dress she kept for Sunday. Kirby wanted to go to college, but he was working because his father couldn't afford to send him away to school.

Outside the storm struck with elemental fury, rain pouring down the windows in a thin sheet. The shades had not been drawn, and Ballard instinctively shivered as lightning threw its savage, shifting flame against the earth and thunder made the house tremble. Storms like this always bothered Ballard. It was another reason for leaving the country.

He pressed his back against the leather chair, pulling hard on his cigar. He tried to relax, tried to ignore the storm. It wouldn't last, he told himself. His mind turned to Bill Worden again, and he wondered how he could gracefully give or lend money to his father-in-law after he was married. He'd have to leave it to Ellen. She could handle her stiff-necked father better than he could.

It was nearly nine when Ellen came in from the dining room. She said, "Supper's finally ready, George."

He threw his cigar stub into the fireplace and put his arm around Ellen as they went into the dining room. She submitted, her body tense, and again he was conscious that something had gone wrong.

Mrs. Worden, standing at the end of the table by her chair, said, "I'm sorry we're late, George. We just couldn't seem to get organized tonight."

"It looks good," he said, his eyes on the table, the silver gleaming in the candlelight. "You shouldn't have gone to all this trouble."

"We were glad to," Mrs. Worden said.

After Ballard had helped Ellen with her chair and taken his place across the table from her, he noticed that Mrs. Worden was wearing her Sunday taffeta. Her face showed the same strain that was in Ellen's.

He mentally cursed all women for their emotions, thinking briefly of Nan who had never, in the time he had known her, given way to her feelings. It was one of the things he had liked about her, probably the reason he had not broken with her sooner than he had.

The meal was perfect, as every meal he had eaten here had been. Fried chicken, mashed potatoes, gravy, strong coffee the way he liked it, and biscuits that were light and fluffy. He was never sure whether Ellen could cook or not, but it didn't make any difference. She wouldn't have to cook after they were married.

This was the first time he had eaten here without Bill Worden being at the table. He wondered if that was what was wrong. Neither Ellen nor her mother ate with the hearty appetite they usually had. Both took only slivers of the three-layer chocolate cake Ellen brought from the kitchen. When at last they were done, Ballard leaned back and reached for a cigar.

"That meal was another masterpiece." He smiled at Ellen. "Were you the artist? Or was it your mother?"

"Both of us, I guess." Ellen rose. "I'll help Mamma with the dishes. You go back and be comfortable, George."

There was nothing to do but return to the parlor and wait. He threw another chunk of pine on the fire and dropped into the leather chair. The worst of the storm was over. He finished his cigar and smoked another, time ribboning out as irritation grew in him. Ellen and her mother had had time to do dishes for a roundup crew. Usually Mrs. Worden insisted that Ellen keep him company, but tonight that was different just as everything else was different.

When Ellen finally came into the parlor, she did not sit on the arm of his chair as was her habit. Instead she drew a stool to the fireplace and sat down, her eyes on the fire.

"It was a terrible storm, wasn't it?" she asked.

She was just making talk, as if they were strangers. "Been coming all day," he said. Silence fell again, uneasy and tense, and because he could not stand it, he cried out, "Ellen what in heaven's name is wrong?"

She looked at him. "George, you know as well as I do. What's going to happen to Daddy tonight?"

So that was it. He had never known Ellen to worry about her father. Or Mrs. Worden, either. Bill Worden had always succeeded in keeping his job and his home separated, and that, Ballard thought, was the way it should be. Someone must have talked to Ellen and her mother after he had been here this afternoon.

"Nothing," he said. "Your dad is a man who can take care of himself."

"But not against everybody," she cried. "We know what people are saying. Maybe you don't realize how gossip travels in this town."

"Ellen, I hate Gunlock," he blurted. "I don't want to stay here. I'd like to take you away and stay away. We'll live in San Francisco. I've been thinking about it. Everybody knows too much about everybody else in this town. We've got a right to live . . ."

She threw out a hand in a gesture of impatience. "Let's be sensible, George. Your business is here and I couldn't leave my folks." She took a long breath. "Mrs. Webb and Mrs. Quinn were here this afternoon. Not long after you left. They told us what's going on. Daddy doesn't talk about things like that, so we hadn't dreamed it was as bad as it is."

"Those two old biddies don't know . . ." He stopped. She was staring at the fire again so he could see only the profile of her face. "What did they tell you?"

"Judge Webb and Doc Quinn wanted to send for a company of the National Guard, but Daddy wouldn't stand for it." She turned to face him again. "George, we might just as well have this out. You could hold the ranchers off, but instead you want to leave town with me. Why, George, why?"

He jumped up, angry because she was close to the truth. Maybe she had guessed. He said harshly, "I don't know what you're talking about. I love you, Ellen. That's why. We've still got time to catch the midnight train."

She shook her head. "I can't go. You ought to know that. If anything happens to Daddy tonight, it will be your fault."

He threw up his hands. "I don't intend to help

184

break Lake out of jail if that's what you're getting at. Sure, I've heard the gossip, but it's lies, Ellen, just lies. If any of my neighbors break the law to help Lake, it won't be because I had anything to do with it."

"But you could help Daddy. You could go down to the jail and stay with him. Or bring your men in from the ranch."

"You know what your dad would do. It'd be like sending for the National Guard." He came to her and knelt beside her. "Let's not quarrel, Ellen. Please. I tell you I've had all of this town and its little people I can stand. Please go away with me. I love you, Ellen. Don't you believe that?"

"I did until tonight," she said slowly. "Now I don't know. I mean, you asking me to run away with you when we were to be married in two weeks anyhow."

He rose and turned away from her. "I might as well go home," he said dully. "If there was anything I could do to help, I'd do it. You ought to know that."

She jumped up and ran to him. He took her into his arms, and for the first time that evening, she wanted to be there, to be held and kissed, her lips hungry for his as they had been from the day he had told her he loved her.

He led her to the couch and they sat down, his arm around her. He felt her tremble. She said, "I'm scared, George. There's so much ugly talk. About Lake and why he came here. I tried not to

185

listen. I didn't want to believe any of it. But tonight . . ."

"You can trust your father to do what must be done," he broke in, "whether you trust me or not."

He waited for her to say she trusted him but she didn't, and for a long time they remained that way in silence, his arm around her, her head on his shoulder. The storm was over except for an occasional spatter of rain against the windows. He wasn't sure it was rain. Maybe just the wind. By this time Lake had his gun. Probably he was gone. Bill Worden might be dead. No, someone would have brought word if that had happened.

Now, more than ever before, Ballard felt the need of a woman's love, the kind Ada Worden gave her husband. But he didn't have it. His love wasn't enough for Ellen, he thought indignantly. The things he could give her weren't enough.

He felt his own weakness, the weakness that had plagued him all his life. He thought of what his grandfather would have said to Ellen. A woman took a man for what he was. She didn't suspect or distrust him. She simply believed in him, and she did what he asked her to do.

He felt no regret about anything he had done. He had simply tried to protect what was his in the only way he could. It was the same with Hogan and Ryman and the others. The farmers were Johnny-come-latelies, land thieves stealing what had been created in a savage wilderness a long time ago by Longhorn Ballard.

If the law wouldn't protect you, you had to do what you could. But he couldn't explain it to Ellen any more than he could explain it to her father, or tell her why he couldn't help Bill Worden. He thought of the understanding that had always been so evident between Ada Worden and her husband, the complete trust. But there was no common ground between him and Ellen. He never realized it before.

Suddenly he pushed her away and rose. "I packed my valise before I came over. I was so sure you'd go." He swallowed. "I thought you felt the same way about me as I felt about you."

He turned toward the hall door, still hoping she'd say she'd go, but she remained where he had left her. Halfway to the door he turned and looked at her. Hell, he should have known. She was mule-stubborn; she was Bill Worden's daughter. She couldn't even give him what Jeannie Mason had given Ed Lake.

He heard the front door slam, heard Ada Worden run along the hall and the murmur of talk. Ballard froze. He recognized Bill Worden's voice. Something had gone wrong with Lake's escape, or Worden wouldn't be here.

The hall door was flung open and Worden came in, his boots covered with mud, his craggy face stone-hard as his eyes met Ballard's. He said, "Ada just told me you asked Ellen to run away with you tonight."

"I thought we'd be married in Salt Lake City . . ."

"You're lying," Worden said. "You never intended to marry her. She'd just be another Nan to you."

"Don't talk to me that way," Ballard shouted. "I love her. I wanted to take her away from . . ."

"But you could have waited two weeks." Ada Worden pushed past her husband. "We worked all day on her wedding dress. We had everything planned, but you couldn't wait. Why, George, why?"

And he had told Ellen her mother would understand. But she was thinking of a big wedding; she wanted to show off before the women of the town. He said, "After all this time, I thought I knew you and Ellen, but we're strangers. I guess it's a good thing this happened."

He stalked past Worden into the hall and took his hat from the rack. He slapped it on his head and opened the door; then he was aware that Bill Worden had followed him. "What is it now?" he cried. "Haven't you done enough to me already?"

"I haven't even started," Worden said. "Ed Lake didn't make it tonight."

Ballard wheeled to the door and went out, Worden behind him. He said in a frightened voice, "Leave me alone."

"Keep walking," Worden said.

"Are you arresting me?"

"No."

"Then damn it, quit bullying me."

Ballard strode down the path to the board-walk, Worden falling into step beside him. As they turned toward Ballard's house, Worden said, "Jeannie Mason got the string to Lake just as you planned and Nan tied the gun to it. Might have worked if Orval Jones hadn't been watching in the hall."

"I don't know anything about it," Ballard muttered, and hurried on.

"Jeannie got the money you paid Lake," Worden said, keeping step with Ballard. "She's gone, figuring on meeting Lake somewhere. Nan decided she couldn't let me and McNamara get shot, so she told me how it was. She showed me the two notes you wrote to Lake."

Ballard walked faster. Worden had no evidence. Worden was just trying to trap him. "I suppose my name was on those notes. That why you think I had anything to do with it?"

They waded the mud of the street intersection and went along the walk to Ballard's place. Worden said, "No, your name wasn't there, but Nan recognized your printing. Want to tell me about it?"

"I would if I knew anything."

"I tried your house a while ago, but you weren't home, so I guessed you'd be with Ellen. I might not have done anything if Ada hadn't told me about you wanting to run off with Ellen.

Now I'm going to."

Worden was talking as coldly as if he were about to slaughter a steer. Fear crawled up Ballard's spine. Worden intended to kill him. He started to run; he got through the gate of the metal fence in front of his house before Worden caught up with him, then he was spun around and a fist smashed him squarely in the face and knocked him down.

Ballard had never been in a fight in his life. He had never needed to, being a Ballard, but Bill Worden was no respecter of persons. Ballard got up and plunged at Worden, swinging wildly, and again a fist caught him, swiveling his head half around, hurting and jarring him. He tried to strike back, but his blows were wasted. Again he went down, and Worden fell on him, pinning him flat on his back in the wet grass. Worden got his hands on Ballard's throat and choked him. Ballard struck at Worden with his fists, futile blows that didn't even sting; he kicked and tried to turn, but now he couldn't even breathe. Worden was an animal, hungry for life. His big thumbs pressed against Ballard's throat; then, with consciousness slipping from Ballard, Worden's grip relaxed. From a great distance his words came to Ballard. "If you ever see Ellen again, I'll kill you. You'd better get out of town and stay out."

Worden rose and strode away. For a time Ballard didn't move. He heard Worden's boots pound on the wet walk as he went away, hard, angry blows on the planks; then the sound was gone. He sat up, breathing hard, and for a time it seemed as if he could not get air back into his lungs. Then it came, and he felt his bruised throat; he brought a hand across his face and felt the warm blood.

He was surprised that he was alive; then he wondered why Worden had not arrested him. There could be only one answer. The sheriff did not have the kind of evidence that would stand up in court. But Worden was like a bull dog. He'd find out from Hogan or some of the others. But if Worden was dead . . . Then his injured pride burst through him like a vivid, singeing flame.

"I'll kill him," he said aloud. "God damn him, I'll kill him."

# Chapter Fourteen

**WORDEN** walked slowly down the hill to the courthouse, weak and ashamed. He had never so completely lost his self-control before, at least not since he had taken office. He had come very close to killing Ballard.

If he were a private citizen, he wouldn't have cared, for George Ballard deserved to die if any man ever did. But Worden was not a private citizen. He had to wait until he had evidence that would hang Ballard.

It was after eleven but in town a few lights still burned: in Worden's and Ballard's houses, in Rigdon's church and the hotel and Casino on Main Street. And in the windows on the second floor of the courthouse. But most of the buildings were dark shapes, scattered in the flat along the creek and on the hill beyond.

Gunlock was asleep. Worden thought of the people who made up the town. Doc Quinn. Judge Webb. Tad Barton. Luke Prentice. A dozen more, men and their wives and their children. To them this was just another night. When they had gone to bed, they had probably wondered if Bill Worden would be alive in the morning. And whether Ed Lake would still be in jail. Probably they hoped he would be, for a public hanging was a macabre show that would attract all of them in the morning, a show they wouldn't want to miss.

He reached the boardwalk that formed a square around the courthouse. The night was not quite as dark as it had been. The clouds were beginning to break away, and here and there a star glittered with cold, distant brilliance.

Suddenly he was aware that someone was coming toward him on the walk. He drew his gun and stepped off the walk into the wet grass. As he waited in the darkness he began to make out that it was not one man but two.

When they were quite close, he called, "Who is it?"

"Sid Lesser," one of them said quickly. And the other, "Fred DeLong."

Worden swore. The damned reporters, prowling around town when they should be in bed. "Get off the street," Worden said harshly. "Want to get shot?"

"No," Lesser said, "but we do want a story. What's up, Sheriff?"

"Get off the street or I'll lock you up. I told you once."

"You said not to come around the jail," Lesser said. "I doubt that you have a law which says a man must stay off the street."

"All right, get shot."

Worden would have gone past them if Lesser hadn't said, "I hear you jailed Ryman."

"That's right."

"Why?"

"My business."

Again Worden would have walked on if Lesser hadn't said, "You're making a mistake, Sheriff. You need a good press if anything goes wrong."

"To hell with you," and this time Worden strode past them and turned along the walk that angled across the courthouse lawn to the front door.

He heard a hymn being sung in Rigdon's church. So the farmers were still in town, still waiting, and he knew no more about their plans than he had when he had left the church hours before. He heard the whistle of the approaching westbound. Midnight! He hadn't realized it was so late. More reporters would be on the train.

A Roman holiday! Like Lesser and DeLong, they'd want a story. They'd have one if Lake broke jail. Or even if he was executed. People would read about it who never heard of Gunlock, read about it because they found some sort of perverse pleasure in the story of a man's violent death.

Worden pulled the door open and went in. So Sid Lesser thought the law needed a good press. But why? The sympathies of all citizens should be with the law. *Should be!* He swore, wondering how many townspeople honestly hoped Lake would get away. To some of them it was a sort of game; they were spectators, and because the odds were against Ed Lake, they were on his side.

But that was wrong. Actually the odds were against Bill Worden and Mike McNamara. It was still nine hours before this would be finally decided. Sid Lesser and Fred DeLong wouldn't understand if he tried to explain how it was. The story was right here, in the uncertainty and the waiting, and the chance that anything could happen in nine hours.

Worden took a long step when he reached the squeaky board in the stairs, missing it, and went on to the second-story hall. No one was in sight, and as he passed the door of his office, he saw that Nan Hogan was waiting. He glanced into the jail. Orval Jones was sitting at the desk, his shotgun and needle gun in front of him.

Worden asked, "Everything all right?"

"Right as rain," Jones said cheerfully.

McNamara lay on the cot, his hat over his face. Now he yanked his hat to one side and sat up. "Anything going on outside?"

"No," Worden said. "Too early."

He went back along the hall to his office and sat down. He said, "Ballard tried to get Ellen to run away with him and take the midnight train."

Nan nodded as if she was not surprised. "He doesn't want to be here in the morning."

Worden picked up his pipe. "I guess you know him better than anyone else."

She nodded gravely, then asked, "Ellen wouldn't go?"

"No."

"Then she doesn't love him, Mr. Worden, and she'll never marry him. If it had been me . . ." She shrugged. "But Ellen's a good girl, raised in a good home, taken care of. Nobody ever gave me anything. Not till I married Lew."

He had found some comfort in this same thought about Ellen, that she had showed tonight she didn't really love Ballard. Still, she would be hurt, and it would take time for her to understand her own feelings. She might blame him. If she did, the gap between them would be wider than ever.

"What did you do to George?" Nan asked.

Worden looked at his bruised knuckles. "I licked hell out of him. Told him to get out of town."

"He won't like that, Mr. Worden." She waited until he lighted his pipe, then added, "He's not a brave man. That's why he hired Lake."

Worden leaned back in his chair, slack-muscled, weariness gripping him. "I don't expect any man to like a beating."

"You still don't understand," she said. "I'm sure no one ever hit him before. He's kind of sick, Mr. Worden. Inside him, I mean. He'll try to kill you, but you won't know it when he does."

"I've got enough things to worry about already," Worden said brusquely. "I'm not afraid of Ballard."

"You should be. You made him the most dangerous man in the county."

Worden shook his head at her, smiling a little.

"I don't think you do know him."

"There's nothing else I can say." She rose. "Are you going to arrest me?"

Worden took his pipe out of his mouth. He should. By her own admission she had tried to help Lake escape. Regretting it later and warning him did not change the facts. But he had no place to keep a woman, and if there was trouble later on, he didn't want her in the building.

"No," he said. "You can go."

"If you see Lew, tell him I'm staying in Jeannie's house." He nodded, and then, after a moment's hesitation, she said, "I'd like for you to give me a gun. A revolver."

"You want me to give you another gun to smuggle to Lake?" Worden said angrily. "What kind of a damn fool do you think I am?"

She bit her lip, staring steadily at him. She said, "You know there is no way I can get a gun to Lake. I've told you before and I'll tell you again. My only concern is for Lew. If you can get him to come to Jeannie's house, I'll keep him there if I have to shoot him in the leg to do it."

He had known her as a straightforward, honest woman. Now, meeting her gaze squarely, he could not doubt her honesty in this. It had taken a good deal of courage to come to him tonight and tell him about Lake having a gun. And only a moment before she had inadvertently told him more about herself than she had intended. She had loved George Ballard and she had lost him, and now, Worden thought, she would protect Lew with fierce possessiveness because he was all she had.

Worden opened a desk drawer and taking out a short-barreled .32, handed it to her. "There are five shells in it."

"Thank you, Mr. Worden." She hesitated, wanting to say something else, but the words would not come to her, and she turned and left the room.

Worden sat there, listening to her heavy steps until they died. He had often been a hunch player, and he had never been wrong. Hunches come out of the deep, unthinking part of a man's mind, stemming, perhaps, from his experience and his knowledge of people. There was an earthy, matter-of-fact quality about Nan that made him trust her. But it was not likely she would get hold of Lew in time.

Worden rose and went into the jail. He took a Winchester from the gunrack and levered a shell into the chamber. He said, "If it's going to come, I figure it'll be in the next two or three hours."

McNamara got up from the cot and rubbed his face. He yawned, glanced at Jones who was still sitting at the desk, and gave Worden a wry grin. "Three of us," he said. "Long odds."

"Yeah," Worden said. "Long odds."

He returned to his office. Then the waiting. He paced around the room, going often to the window to stare into the blackness. He could see nothing. He lifted the window and listened. No sound except the night wind breathing through the poplars. The air was still damp, still tangy with sage smell, but now the sky had cleared and the stars were out. He wondered if anyone had ever counted them.

He lowered the window. Small, so damned small. The county. Gunlock. The courthouse. He and Mike McNamara and Orval Jones. Small when you thought of all eternity that lay out there beyond the window, the stars and the boundless space that was sky.

And yet the thing they were doing was big. Judge Webb and Doc Quinn had known that and they had said so, not thinking he had the qualities it took to do a job of this size. He wasn't sure he did, but he was sure of one thing. If he died tonight, no one else was capable of doing what must be done. McNamara was the only man who would even try, and he was too young.

Stature comes with age and experience. It was something in other men's minds. The farmers did not trust him; the ranchers feared him because he stood in their way. But both respected him because they knew what he would and could do, and that was his biggest asset.

One hour. Two. Then three. Dragging hours. The concept of time, like size, was often a matter of comparison. He should be asleep, unconscious of the mechanical marking of seconds and minutes, but there was no sleep for him. Not for six hours. Now the six hours loomed ahead, an eternity of waiting.

The front door opened and closed. Worden grabbed his Winchester from the desk and ran into the hall, calling, "Mac. Orval." They appeared at once, Jones with his shotgun, McNamara with a .30-.30.

Then Worden looked down the stairs and took a long, sighing breath. "It's Ada," he said. "Go on back."

She came up the stairs, her head tipped back, her smile for him. She was carrying a lunch basket in her right hand. Now she waved with her free hand, calling, "I thought you'd be hungry."

"You shouldn't be here," he said, unable to keep the worry out of his voice.

She reached the hall and taking his arm, walked with him into his office. "You're not afraid, are you, Bill?"

"No," he lied.

He had never told her he was afraid. He often thought she was convinced he was incapable of feeling fear. She set the basket on the desk and took out a plate of sandwiches and a jar of coffee. He stood there, looking at her, suddenly choked up with his feeling for her and wishing he had the talent for expressing himself. But she knew. She lifted her eyes to his and he was sure she knew.

"I brought enough for Mac," she said.

"Orval's with Mac," Worden said. "I'll take some of the sandwiches to them."

"And the coffee," she said. "I brought a

couple of extra cups. I thought someone else might be here."

He was gone only a moment, returning with a jar of coffee half empty. She took it from him and filled the cup on his desk. He ate a sandwich and drank the coffee, unable to keep his eyes away from her.

Embarrassed, she asked, "What is it, Bill?"

"I just like to look at you," he said. "What's the weather like outside?"

"The sky's clear. It's warmed up some, I think."

He reached for another sandwich. "How's Ellen?"

"She's in bed. I'll have to get back to her."

"You think Ballard will try to see her again?"

"I don't know. Anyhow, I don't want to leave her alone." She paused, her face grave, then added, "You've never said so, but I've known for a long time that you didn't want her to marry George. I never knew why until tonight."

"I figured it was Ellen's right to pick her husband," he said. "I might have been wrong."

"You weren't, but that won't help Ellen." Ada shook her head. "In time she'll realize she didn't really love him, but right now she's all mixed up. We've got to be patient with her. It will be hard to explain. To her friends, I mean."

Pride, he thought sourly. A big wedding. The dress made. Everyone knowing. Now all the women in town would have a new topic for gossip. Ellen could not help noticing their stares and smirks and knowing what was being said behind her back.

Ada picked up the basket. "There are a lot of men around the courthouse. I didn't know whether you'd seen them or not."

He had a sandwich halfway to his mouth when she said that. Now he dropped it back onto the plate. "What men?"

"It was too dark to recognize many of them. Orson was the one who stopped me. Then Preacher Rigdon came up. And Ben Smith. Don't get angry about it, Bill. They were very courteous and let me go on as soon as they found out who I was."

The farmers! A lot of men, she'd said. Probably all of them, forty or more. He said, "I'll go out with you."

"No, you . . ."

"Come on," he said, and jerked his head toward the door.

"I shouldn't have told you," she said, exasperated. "They aren't doing anything. Just standing there."

"Come on," he repeated.

She sighed, and went with him. He could not see anyone when he left the courthouse. He eased his gun out of the holster and let it settle back. There was no way of knowing what they meant to do, and he was doubtful that they would tell him.

When he and Ada reached the poplars, a man called, "That you, Sheriff?"

It was Ben Smith. Other men moved toward him as he said, "Yeah, it's me."

"Your wife will be safe," Smith said. "You should know we respect a woman, Sheriff."

"Go along, Ada," Worden said.

He stood there while she walked away. Yes, he should have known she'd be safe. But he didn't like it. Half a dozen men stood around him. All of them were armed, but the star-shine was not strong enough to see the expression on their faces.

Then he made out Rigdon's wide, square figure, and he shouted, "Speak up, Preacher. What are you doing here? It's after three."

"Don't ask me," Rigdon said, his voice heavy with bitterness. "I'm not running this shebang."

"I am," Smith said. "It was my boy who was murdered. That's why I'm a sort of temporary chairman."

"What are you doing here?"

"Taking in the night air," Smith said softly. "There's no law against that. Go on back, Sheriff. We mean you no harm."

"Damn it, what are you doing here?"

"Tell him, Ben," Orson said.

"All right, I'll tell him. You're a proud man, Sheriff. You did not ask for help, but we're giving it anyhow. We propose to see to it that Lake hangs, legal and proper."

So that was it. They had listened to what he had said to them, listened and been convinced. He said, "All right, stand out here if you want to, but don't come inside."

"We don't aim to," Smith said.

Worden returned to the courthouse. He told McNamara and Jones about it. Jones said, "Hell, I can go to bed, if that's the way it is."

"No," Worden said sharply.

"What happens if Hogan and Jiggs Larribee and the rest of 'em ride in?" McNamara asked.

"Hell pops," Worden said.

He moved a chair into the hall and sat down at the head of the stairs, his Winchester across his lap. He was bone-tired. It was an ache in his legs, and his arms were so heavy they threatened rebellion against his command, and suddenly he was aware that his fingers had relaxed their hold on the rifle and it was starting to slide off his lap. He grabbed it, realizing he had dropped off to sleep and suddenly angry at his weakness.

He got up and walked back and forth along the hall until he was thoroughly awake. He sat down again, and once more time dragged out, even slower now. He did not understand why the cowmen hadn't come, and he had no idea what he would do if they did. Then, as the minutes passed, the hope grew in him that they wouldn't come.

Suddenly the door at the foot of the stairs was slammed open. Worden called, "Mac. Orval. Get out here." He stood up, his Winchester on the ready.

Ben Smith came into view in the hall below them. He looked up at Worden, and McNamara and Jones who flanked him. Smith said quietly, "I heard what you said about staying outside, but I thought you'd want to know that a bunch of riders are coming into town from the north."

Worden glanced at McNamara who nodded. The deputy said, "I almost gave them up."

"Yeah, so did I," Worden said. "Stay here, Orval. Mac, come with me."

# Chapter Fifteen

**THIS** was the ebb time with night almost gone, the hour when new life was most likely to be born, when old, spent life was most likely to flicker out the way a low flame dies when the fuel is gone. Worden had heard Doc Quinn say that many times, and now, with the cowmen riding in, Worden thought it must be true. Even the stars seemed a little paler, their light a little weaker.

Worden asked, "Can you keep your men under control?"

"If there is trouble," Ben Smith answered, "it will be of their making, not ours."

"Rigdon?"

Smith was silent for a long moment, the incoming riders closer now. Then he said in a low tone, "The Parson will be leaving the country soon."

An indirect answer, but a significant one. Worden did not press the question. He wished he knew what had happened after he had left the church with Tremaine. He could guess. As Tremaine had said, there was something wrong with Rigdon, and Smith and Orson and the rest must finally have discovered it. When they had, Rigdon's control over them was gone.

McNamara stood on one side of Worden, Ben Smith on the other. Farther down the walk were the others, silent, motionless men who stood waiting. The riders passed the courthouse square, vague shapes in the darkness, the horses' hoofs making sucking sounds in the street mud.

This was not the way Worden had expected it to go. He had supposed the ranchers would attack the jail, but they went on toward the Casino, apparently unaware of the farmers' presence. Worden said, "Mac and me will have a talk with them. What will you boys be doing while we're talking?"

"Nothing," Smith said.

"We can't walk off . . ." McNamara began.

"Walk as far as you want to," Smith said. "We will not risk our lives and our future in Grant County, Worden. Not to hang a man who will hang in another five hours. You said that in the church. It made sense."

"Come on, Mac," Worden said, and started toward the Casino.

McNamara was silent until they waded the mud at the intersection and were on the boardwalk that led to the saloon. Then he burst out, "I never saw you fall into a trap like this before. What do you think Smith got us out of the courthouse for?"

Worden was silent for a moment. He had never been so tired before in his life, tired of waiting, tired of uncertainty, tired of being afraid. It was almost twenty-four hours since he had slept.

He remembered how it had been, waking with the harsh sunlight in his eyes, Ada in bed beside him. The trust that both the stockmen and farmers had given him had been a source of pride to him, and the loss of that trust had hurt him.

Now he was sure he had restored the farmers' faith in him when he had talked to them in church, restored it in spite of all that Preacher Rigdon could do. Perhaps he was taking some risk now, but mistrust begot mistrust, and conversely trust begot trust. So he was doing the only thing he could do.

"I know what you're thinking, but I figure you're wrong," Worden said finally. "Now I want you to go around to the back door of the Casino. I'll wait thirty seconds, then I'm going in through the front. Just cover me. No shooting unless they start it. Savvy?"

"I savvy we're committing suicide," McNamara grunted.

But he went, into the pit-blackness of the narrow passage between the Casino and the building beside it, splashing through ankle-deep puddles that remained after the storm. Worden waited at the corner of the building. He checked his gun and replaced it in leather, then edged toward a window and peered in. Fourteen of them, lined up along the bar as they listened to Leo Roos.

Worden stepped past the window and went on to the bat wings. He stopped, glancing at the row of horses racked at the hitch pole. He still had no explanation for the cowmen's delay in coming to town, and he had no way of knowing whether that delay meant anything or not. But there was one thing that encouraged him. The men inside were little fry, men like Lew Hogan. Not one of Ballard's Lazy B hands was here. It would be a different story if Jiggs Larribee and his men were with the others.

Worden waited until he was sure more than thirty seconds had passed, then he shouldered through the bat wings. He said, "Howdy, boys."

Lew Hogan stood at the end of the line. He was the one to watch, Worden thought, for he was the only leader among them, not because he had any inherent talent for leadership, but because he possessed a dogged, unyielding stubbornness that held weaker men in line.

They wheeled to face Worden, as shocked by his appearance as the farmers had been when he had walked down the church aisle. Again a sense of predestined failure was in Worden. He had been on solid ground when he'd talked to the farmers because the law had delegated to him the very thing they wanted done, but these men had met tonight with deliberate intent to put aside the law.

Worden strode toward Hogan. It took no more than ten seconds to reach the bar; he saw the hard set of Hogan's square face, and he had a bad moment when he thought Hogan was going for his gun. One shot would set it off. He could get Hogan, but he couldn't get all of them.

The timing was perfect. Before Worden reached the bar, McNamara came through the back door, calling, "Stand pat, boys. Keep your hand away from your gun, Poling."

McNamara's gun was in his hand. He was not wearing a hat. His red hair stuck up above his forehead with the bristling fierceness of porcupine quills. He had not shaved for two days. He was never a handsome man, and now there was a deadly ugliness about him that could not be taken lightly.

At any other time it would have been comical. Fourteen heads, fifteen with the bartender's, turned at the first word McNamara spoke, swiveling on their shoulders in a unison that might have come from long practice. Then, with that same precision, they swung back, eyes pinned on Worden's face.

"Leo says you've got Jess in jail," Hogan burst out. "Who'n hell do you think you are?"

"The law," Worden said. "He drew a gun on me. I'll jail any of you who try it."

"And you'll be a dead man," Hogan shouted. "You're turning Jess loose. You hear?"

"I expect to." Worden stood five feet from Hogan, his gaze running down the line of faces and returning to Hogan's. "Lew, your wife wants to see you. She's in Jeannie Mason's house."

"You're lying. Nan's home. You're just trying to worry me about something that ain't so."

Worden shook his head. "I'm not lying. She and Jeannie . . ." He stopped, realizing that if he

210

made a public statement of Nan's part in George Ballard's scheme to free Lake, he'd have to arrest her, and he told her he wouldn't. "They got Lake's valise out of his hotel room. It had the money Ballard paid him for the killings. I owe Nan something for fetching me the letters Ballard wrote to Lake, so I'm overlooking what she did to help Jeannie get the money."

They were stunned. That puzzled him until he realized they might not have known it was Ballard who had paid Lake. The part these men had in the murders was a question in his mind, and had been from the first. He hoped he would never have the answer. Ballard was the guilty man.

Halfway down the bar Dick Poling said, "That's damned queer talk, coming from the man who's gonna be George Ballard's father-in-law."

"I won't be," Worden said harshly. "He had a cute scheme to get Lake out of jail, but it didn't work. Lake will hang because the law says he's got to hang. I know what you boys figure on doing. Don't try it. You've got families. You'd be fools to make your wives widows for a back-shooting killer like Lake."

Rage had been growing in Hogan, his face getting redder by the second. Now he was breathing so hard he was panting. He yelled, "You're on the farmers' side. That's why you're lying about my wife being in town. And about Mr. Ballard. He's one of us. Lake was on our side, too, and we ain't gonna let him hang because he kept a gang of sodbusting farmers from stealing our land."

The rest nodded, their faces hard-set by determination. Worden felt as if he were butting his head against a solid wall, and again the feeling of failure was in him. It was natural for them to think and feel this way. They were innocents caught in a trap that Ballard had set. He could not change them, but he had to try.

"I don't make the law, Lew," Worden said patiently. "I didn't sit on the jury that convicted Lake. I didn't sentence him to hang. He made an appeal to a higher court and lost. The governor refused to step in. So he's got to hang, and there's nothing you boys can do to stop it."

"We'll stop it," Hogan shouted. "And I say you're on their side. You . . ."

He choked, unable to say anything more, and then, feeling utterly frustrated and helpless, and made a little crazy by the waiting, he could think of nothing except to beat Worden down with his fists.

Hogan drove at Worden, swinging a wild uppercut from his knees. Again McNamara yelled, "Stand pat, the rest of you." Worden had seen the fury grow and break in Hogan, and he was ready for the man's attack. He pivoted, Hogan's blow missing by a full six inches. Hogan, off balance and helpless for a second, was wide open. Worden caught him with a right on the side of the head, rocking it, then a left to the chin. It was like chopping down a giant, stubby pine. Hogan fell against the bar, his head striking hard.

"No more of that," Worden said. "I didn't come here for trouble. I came to keep you boys out of it. Right now you're hating me, but in another week after you've had time to think about it, you'll see it different."

Hogan sat where he had fallen, a little dazed, a hand rubbing his face. He muttered, "We'll never see it different, and you ain't changed nothing. Not a damned thing. We're taking Lake away from you."

Dick Poling, a lanky man who had a wife and six children, and an outfit not much bigger than Hogan's, jabbed a forefinger at Worden. He said, "You made some tall talk about Mr. Ballard. What are you gonna do about it?"

Worden sighed. Here was his weakness. If Ballard wasn't arrested, these men and everyone else in town would say it was because of Ellen. He said the only thing he could. "When I get the kind of evidence that holds up in court, Ballard will be arrested." He paused, his gaze on Hogan's face, then he added, "And maybe you boys will, too."

Hogan pulled himself upright, a hand on the bar. He said thickly, "You want a big hanging. That it, Worden?"

"No. All I want from you is your word you won't do anything to stop Lake's hanging." But they could not give him their word. He saw that at once, and he wondered if it was their sense of guilt that held them here, staring bleakly at him. He said, "Then I'll have to take your guns. You'll get them back right after the hanging. Lay them on the bar. Leo, find a sack."

Worden moved back, watching them closely, not sure they would surrender their guns. But they looked at McNamara who still had them covered, and obeyed. Leo Roos tossed a gunny sack to McNamara who dropped the guns into it. He circled the ranchers, the sack in his left hand, gun in his right.

"You're coming with me, Lew," Worden said.

"You arresting me?" Hogan demanded.

"No," Worden said. "I just want to deliver Jess to you."

A purple bruise had formed on the side of Hogan's face where Worden had hit him. He stared sullenly at Worden, not moving, his stubborn will unchanged by anything that had happened. When Worden looked at Poling and the others, he saw that it was the same with all of them. He might just as well have stayed in the courthouse for all the good he had done.

Worden backed to the door, jerking his head at Hogan who followed. They went into the street, and a moment later McNamara joined them. The stars were fading now, the first opalescent light of dawn appearing along the eastern horizon.

They trudged along the walk toward the courthouse, across the muddy intersection, and when they reached the courthouse square, Ben Smith appeared, asking, "What's going to happen, Sheriff?"

"Nothing," Worden said. "Mac's got their guns."

He hoped it was true that nothing would happen. But the execution was still more than four hours away. He had not learned why they were so late coming to town, or how they planned to free Lake. As far as the guns were concerned, they could find more. Actually he had accomplished nothing by taking them, but he hoped Ben Smith did not realize that.

They walked on toward the front door of the courthouse, past the three Smith boys, past Rigdon, past Orson. None of them spoke. When they reached the courthouse, Worden felt no more assurance than he had when he'd left the church after talking to the farmers. He thought as he so often did that human behavior was never predictable, seldom conforming to logic, dictated by strong emotion rather than cool reason.

Inside the courthouse Hogan demanded, "What are the damned farmers doing here?"

"Making sure you boys behave," Worden answered.

"We ain't scared of no hay shakers," Hogan said.

That was true, Worden thought. The fact that the cowmen were outnumbered almost three to one wouldn't stop them. He had never known a cowboy who didn't think he was worth ten settlers when it came to a finish fight.

They climbed the stairs, the loose board squeaking under foot. Worden called, "It's us, Orval." Jones stood in the hall, shotgun in his hands, and when he saw who it was, he began to tremble.

"Sure glad to see you, Sheriff," Jones said, his voice quavering. "Why I ever figured I wanted to be a deputy is something I don't know."

"That's what I thought," McNamara said.

"Get Jess, Mac," Worden ordered, and waited in the office with Hogan and Jones until the deputy returned with Ryman.

"You're free," Worden said. "I fetched Lew along. I figured he'd want to hear what you had to say."

Ryman gave him a sour grin. "You're a smart hombre, Sheriff." He looked at Hogan. "Where the hell you been all night?"

"Waiting for you to get back," Hogan said. "We didn't want to show up in town if Ed had got away."

Ryman turned to Worden. "There's something I didn't tell you. Ballard told Jiggs Larribee to stay out of town. He said he'd see that Lake got out of the jug, so I rode in to find out."

"We've still got a job to do," Hogan said.

"Not for that bastard," Ryman said. "That's why the sheriff is smart. He wanted me to find out what kind of a hairpin Lake is. I did, too. He almost got away, but he didn't have time to bother with me. After they fetched him back, he spent the rest of the night cussing me and

Ballard. You, too, Lew. Even Jeannie."

"We don't need your help," Hogan said sourly. "Go on home."

Hogan whirled and stomped out. Ryman glanced at Worden, shrugged, and followed. Worden hesitated, wondering about the farmers. This was still too tricky to take any chances. He caught up with Hogan and Ryman at the door and walked out of the building with them. He called, "Smith."

Ben Smith ran across the grass to him. "What's up?"

"Let these boys through," Worden said.

Smith hesitated, his Winchester on the ready as he considered this. "All right," he grunted finally. "There's a bunch of reporters out here wanting to see you."

"Keep them out," Worden said.

He waited until Hogan and Ryman left the courthouse square and crossed the intersection. The light was stronger now. He glanced at the gallows, gaunt and tall, a silent portent of death, then turned and went back inside.

When he reached the jail office, McNamara said, "Damn a stubborn man. That Hogan's a mule if I ever saw one."

"I hope Nan gets hold of him," Worden said.

"She can't stop him," McNamara said. "Nothing can stop him. All of 'em but Ryman will side him, too. They don't have no chance, but they'll try, damn 'em, they'll try."

"They've got a chance if they can get Ballard

217

to send for Larribee," Worden said. "They might talk Larribee into coming anyhow."

McNamara swore. He asked accusingly, "Why didn't you lock Hogan up?"

"You know why," Worden said irritably.

He was ashamed for letting his temper sharpen his voice. McNamara was as tired as he was. He could see it in the deputy's face, a nervous fatigue that was worse than any physical tiredness could ever be.

He went out into the hall and stood by the east window, watching the day come, color spreading slowly above the ridges, first with pastel softness, then the sharp scarlet of the sunrise. Mist rose from the ground, white and eerie with shifting tendrils that drifted with the breeze, then the sun was a red arc above the solid line of hills.

But Worden was only partly conscious of what he saw. He was thinking of McNamara's stupid question that wasn't so stupid if you looked at reality instead of the theory of this thing men called law. You waited until a rule was broken, even if it was nothing more than having a gun pulled on you as Jess Ryman had done.

So you were helpless until an overt act was committed. It might mean your life, but that was the only way you could play it, and it gave the other side all the trumps. Man hadn't moved very far out of the wilderness, not nearly far enough, and he wondered if there would ever be a day when the law would be written so murder could be prevented.

He swore, feeling weariness in every bone and nerve of his body. He was like a man standing at the edge of a precipice, the siren fingers of sleep reaching up to pull him down, then he thought of George Ballard, and he was fully awake at once.

Worden had no illusions about the evidence he had against Ballard, but if he arrested the man, everyone in the county would know what he was, and perhaps he could be destroyed that way. In that moment Worden made his decision. Even at the risk of appearing foolish in court, he would arrest Ballard as soon as the hanging was over.

# Chapter Sixteen

**THE** Chinaman habitually opened his restaurant early. Tremaine's dining room offered better meals, so it was at this hour and after eight o'clock at night that the Chinaman did most of his business. Worden sent Orval Jones out for his breakfast, and told him to bring a tray back for Lake.

Worden watched from his office window, wondering if the farmers who still surrounded the courthouse would try to keep Jones from going through their line. He saw Ben Smith stop Jones, then let him go on. Worden remained by the window, his eyes on the gallows that threw a long, gaunt shadow across the lawn, but actually he was not seeing the gallows, for his mind was on what lay ahead.

At this hour, almost seven now, he still had no way of knowing what would happen when he took Lake out of his cell and they walked across the yard to the scaffold. There was a protection of sorts here inside the courthouse; there would be none outside.

He wanted to believe the ranchers had lost their chance when daylight had come, but he knew that was wishful thinking. Anything could happen yet. On the other hand, he was convinced there would be no trouble from the farmers. They had ceased to be a danger when Rigdon had lost his power over them.

It was a strange thing, a sort of miracle, for Ben Smith had not been an important man in the community. You would have thought that one of the others, Orson perhaps, would have been picked as a leader. You would have thought, too, that Ben Smith would have supported Rigdon in attacking the jail and making sure Lake was hanged.

But all of this simply supported Worden's theory that human behavior was never predictable. Smith was the most level-headed man among the farmers. The struggle with the cowmen would not end with Lake's execution. Perhaps it would never end in a community like this, but Smith recognized the farmers' need for law, and that the surest way to destroy their one support was to attack the law.

What would happen after the hanging? Well, one thing was sure. The Smith family still lived on the quarter section they had taken north of the creek. Others would follow. It was a reasonable guess that by fall the bulk of George Ballard's range would be settled and his ranch destroyed. Eventually his neighbors, Hogan and Ryman and the rest, would see their grass go the same way.

Grant County had always been a stock country. The farmers south of the creek had not changed the basic economy, but in time they would. Worden hated to see the change come. He liked the county the way it had been, but his personal feelings had nothing to do with the issue.

The law said the farmers had a right to settle on open range, and anything the stockmen did to keep the range from being settled would put them outside the law. But they refused to accept that fact, and it was unlikely Ed Lake's execution would make them accept it.

Jones came in with Lake's tray. Worden went with McNamara when the deputy took Lake's breakfast to him and unlocked the cell door and set the tray inside. Lake sat on his bunk, his head in his hands. Now he looked up and began to curse them. Then he cursed Jeannie because she had left town and their plan had failed.

McNamara said, "Shut that up, or I'll come in there and lay a gun barrel across your head."

McNamara stepped back and locked the cell door. Lake rose and came to the bars. "You damned star toters. I should have shot both of you when I came to town. I never did like your breed."

"And we never liked yours," Worden said. "Come on, Mac."

When they were back in the office and the corridor door shut and locked, McNamara said, "He didn't quit hoping till the sun came up. Now he knows he's a goner."

"Go get your breakfast, Mac," Worden said. "Orval can stay here."

Worden returned to his office. Moving to the window, he saw a knot of men, half a dozen or more, standing in front of Ben Smith and arguing with him. Reporters, Worden guessed. He recognized Sid Lesser and Fred DeLong. He didn't know the others. Finally, in disgust, they turned and left.

They had to have their story, Worden thought. Not just the story of the hanging, but all that went on behind the scene. What had happened to the ranchers' plan to break Lake out? Why hadn't the farmers taken Lake out and hanged him as they were supposed to have done? And what about Ballard who was engaged to marry the sheriff's girl?

Worden could see the headlines. He wheeled from the window and sat down at his desk. He filled his pipe, his mind reluctantly turning to Ballard. The man was still his problem, both officially and personally.

Worden tried not to think of Ellen, but she kept crowding into his mind. She knew now what Ballard was, but would it make any difference? Would she be like Jeannie Mason, refusing to believe what she knew, or wanting to marry him even if she did believe?

Worden lighted his pipe, and because he could not sit still, he got up and paced around his office. He could not keep the thought of Ballard from running through his mind. What would Ballard do?

Nan had said he'd try to kill Worden. But he

was a coward. Nan had recognized that. She'd said he was kind of sick, down inside him. But there were different kinds of sickness, different degrees of insanity, if you want to call it that.

Rigdon, brutal and sadistic who had wanted to do the hanging. Lake, with his perverted sense of values that had permitted him to take money in exchange for a man's life. Hogan, so bound by what he considered loyalty that he would have risked everything to free Lake. Jeannie and Nan, sick because of love, so sick they had done a thing they would never have done under other circumstances.

And always Ellen. He jammed his pipe into his pocket. Of all the fears which had plagued him through these tortured hours, this was the worst — that Ellen might hate him because of what he would do to Ballard.

He sat down at his desk again, thinking of what Nan had said about Ballard. "He'll try to kill you, but you won't know it when he does." If Ballard did try, Worden would have the evidence he needed, if he were still alive. That might be the solution. It would at least bring Ballard into the open.

Worden heard McNamara come up the stairs. He stepped into the hall. "I guess I'll get my breakfast."

McNamara nodded, his face showing his weariness. "Go ahead."

Worden went down the stairs and outside into the bright morning sunshine. He walked to the street, spoke to Ben Smith and went on, feeling the farmers' eyes on him. They had kept their cordon around the courthouse, ten or more men on a side, all armed, waiting.

Worden ordered flapjacks and coffee, but he couldn't eat. He drank his coffee, dropped a coin on the counter, and went back into the street. The reporters were there, Lesser demanding, "What about it, Sheriff? Are the farmers deputies?"

"You can call them that," Worden said.

He would have gone on if they hadn't made a solid block in front of him. "We've got a right to see Lake," Lesser said angrily. "We want an interview with him."

"No interview," Worden said. "You can watch the hanging. That's your story."

"The hell it is, young DeLong shouted, and grabbed Worden's arm. "We can't find out anything. What are you trying to do, muzzle the press?"

Worden yanked his arm free, sending DeLong spinning. He almost fell, and then, regaining his balance, he jumped at Worden, but the others caught him and held him. Worden knew how DeLong felt, how all of them felt. They had a job to do, and they were furious because it seemed to them he was keeping them from doing it.

"Lake's going to hang," Worden said. "I tell you that's your story."

"We heard a company of National Guard was

being sent from the capital," Lesser said.

"Gossip," Worden said, and walked past them and went on to the courthouse.

When he reached Smith, the farmer said, "The cowmen left town while you were eating, all but Hogan. What are they up to now?"

Worden stared at Smith, seeing the worry and the fear that was in the man, and it occurred to him that regardless of their numbers, the farmers would be no real protection if the ranchers, reinforced by Jiggs Larribee and his crew, made a headlong attack just as Lake mounted the scaffold. There was still time for Larribee to reach town. Perhaps Ballard had changed his orders.

Fear was in Worden just as it was in Smith, fear of the unknown, fear of what might happen, and he could not give the farmers any assurance it wouldn't happen. He said irritably, "How the hell would I know what they're up to?"

"They've gone after Larribee and his men, and I think you know it." Rigdon had come up behind Worden. "If you let Lake get away now, we'll tar and feather you. We'll run you out of town."

Worden turned to study Rigdon's square, set face. He was sick, all right, sick with frustration, sick with his unnatural hunger to take Lake's life. "You'll be running ahead of me, Rigdon. Keep that in mind."

Worden went into the courthouse. McNamara met him in the hall. "Harris is here, but Lake won't see him."

"We can't do anything about that," Worden said.

He strode past McNamara into his office. He looked at his watch. Ten minutes after eight. Lake was probably counting the minutes he had left, probably still hoping that what he called the "right side" would get him off.

Harris came in. He said, "Sheriff, Lake asked for pen and paper while you were gone." He dropped an envelope on the desk. It was addressed to Jeannie Mason, Santa Fe, Territory of New Mexico. Luck, Worden thought. He could find Jeannie if he needed her to testify against Ballard. She would, he thought, because she would blame Ballard for not freeing Lake.

She could tell the court about Ballard lending her the five hundred dollars. That would help, for any jury from Grant County knew how Ballard ran his bank. They would understand that such a loan would never have been made unless Ballard had his own reason for making it.

Harris cleared his throat. "I have met many evil men, Mr. Worden, but never one as evil as Lake. He wrote this letter to Jeannie and gave it to McNamara to mail, then he cursed her and called her a whore." Harris shook his head as if it was beyond his comprehension. "Think of it, Mr. Worden, the only person who wanted to help him because she loved him."

"I know." Worden motioned to the letter. "I'll take care of this."

When Harris left the room, Worden moved to

the window. Evil, all right, but was Lake any more evil than Ballard? Or did evil, like sickness, come in degrees? If it did, to Worden's way of thinking, Ballard was far worse than Lake.

Already the crowd was gathering, mostly townspeople, forming a circle around the gallows. They had come to see a show, Worden thought savagely. Women and children as well as men, people he knew, people he had regarded as decent folks. But there was something unclean about this. What kind of parents would let their children watch a hanging?

A man was running toward the courthouse, but when he reached the boardwalk, one of the farmers stopped him. It was Lew Hogan. Then Worden remembered Ben Smith saying Hogan had not been with the cowmen when they had left town.

Hogan started toward the courthouse, but two farmers grabbed him and held him, shaking him with unnecessary roughness. Hogan lashed out with a fist, knocking a man sprawling, then a farmer struck him and Hogan went down. When he got to his feet, two of them caught his arm and held him.

Worden raised a window and leaning out, yelled, "Stop it. Let Hogan through."

Rigdon, running toward Hogan, swung around. "That sounds like you, Worden. It'll give you an excuse to let Lake escape."

Worden pulled his gun. He aimed it at Rigdon, and for a terrible second he fought an almost uncontrollable impulse to kill the man. Ben Smith cried out, "Don't do it, Sheriff."

"Let Hogan through," Worden shouted. "Let him through, I tell you."

Smith said something, and the men who were holding Hogan released their grip. He ran on toward the courthouse. Worden remained there, his gun covering Rigdon, until he heard Hogan coming up the stairs, then he drew back and closed the window. He swung around as Hogan came in.

"Nan." Hogan sat down, breathing hard, his face contorted with fear. "Where is she?"

"I don't know. Take it easy, Lew. Nobody would hurt her."

Hogan wiped sweat from his face. "I didn't believe what you said about Nan waiting for me in Jeannie's house. I thought she was home." He swallowed and licked dry lips. "After me'n Jess left here, we went to the Casino. Jess said to let Ed hang. Said he was a son-of-a-bitch who deserved to die. We argued awhile, most of us still trying to figure out how to save his neck. Then Leo remembered Nan had given him a note for me. It was Nan's writing, all right. Said she was at Jeannie's."

Hogan slumped forward. "Well, I got worried finally, so I went up to Jeannie's house. Nan had been there. Left another note that said I was to wait for her. I did, but she didn't show up. I got to thinking about Ballard. She used to be in love with him. I went to his house. The housekeeper wouldn't let me in, but I shoved her out of the door and looked all over the house. Nan wasn't there."

"Ballard?"

"He wasn't there, neither." Hogan got up and sat down again. "What'll I do, Sheriff? You think she ran off with him?"

"No. Lew, I'm not sure you deserve Nan, but there's one thing you can count on. She loves you. She wouldn't run off with Ballard or anyone." Hogan didn't move. He just sat there, staring at Worden with eyes that did not see. Worden said, "Your friends left town a while ago. You reckon they went after Larribee?"

"Mebbe. We thought about that. Figured on telling Jiggs that Ballard had changed his mind and for him to come in with his boys. We were gonna take Lake just after you left the courthouse." Hogan had answered without thinking. He had no capacity for thought now. Only one thing mattered. He cried out, "What'll I do, Sheriff? Where will I look for Nan?"

Worden could give the man no answer, so he said nothing. McNamara called from the doorway, "Time to go, Bill."

"I guess it is," Worden said, and left his office.

# Chapter Seventeen

**NAN** Hogan's conscience had always been conveniently elastic, but as she climbed the hill to Jeannie Mason's house after leaving a note for Lew in the Casino, she knew it was not elastic enough to allow her to stand by and let Bill Worden be murdered. She went in and lighted the lamp and sat down. She stared at the oak table with the glass balls at the base of its legs. But there was no desire in her now to own it.

For the first time in her life she had the power to save a man's life or let him be killed. It was a new problem to her, and she didn't know what to do. She kept telling herself it was none of her business, but she knew she was simply trying to excuse herself for not doing something she should do.

Actually Nan had never given much thought to questions of right or wrong. She had lived as immediate circumstances demanded. But this was different. No one would blame her if Bill Worden was shot and killed by George Ballard. They wouldn't know. But she would, and she could never forget.

She stared at the gun Worden had given her. She'd lied to him, for she'd had no intention of using it to keep Lew here in Jeannie's house.

Lew was a grown man. If what he called loyalty was going to get him into trouble, he'd have to get into trouble. She wasn't going to do anything more for him.

Probably Worden would not see Lew, but the bartender in the Casino would. The note she had given him would bring Lew here. He might come any time. If she was going to do anything about Ballard, she'd better go before Lew came. He'd tell her she was crazy, that she owed nothing to Worden.

She got up and going into Jeannie's bedroom, rummaged around in the bureau drawers until she found pencil and paper. She wrote a note to Lew, telling him to wait until she got back. Probably he wouldn't, but he might wait for a time, maybe long enough to spoil whatever plan he and the others had made to get Lake out of jail. Then she blew out the lamp and left the house.

As she walked to Ballard's place, she thought how people misjudged Bill Worden. Put a star on a man and give him authority, and he'll step on a lot of toes if he's an honest man. That was Worden's trouble.

She knew what was said about Worden. She'd heard Lew say it many times. Bill Worden was as tough as an old boot. Arguing with him was like butting your head against the side of a house. He saw things his way; he did things his way, and you might as well save your wind.

Maybe they were right when it came to a principle Worden believed in, but they were wrong about the little things, questions of human kindness. He had been kind to Jeannie, and that had been a mistake because she had taken advantage of him. And he had been kind to Nan tonight.

He could have put her in jail, but he hadn't. As she trudged through the mud at the intersection and went on along the walk to Ballard's house, she knew that was the real reason she was doing this. If she didn't, she would never be able to live with herself.

She turned through the gate of the metal fence that surrounded the Ballard house, thinking how she had once dreamed of living here, having someone to do her work, giving parties and being accepted by the other women of town. Mrs. Quinn. Mrs. Webb. Mrs. Barton. Yes, even Mrs. Worden.

But she wouldn't have fitted. It was better this way, living in a cabin and working like a man and being so much in love with Lew that she'd even tried to help Ed Lake get out of jail.

She walked through the wet grass to the cast-iron deer in the yard. She stood behind it, studying the big house. There was a light in the front hall. Another in Ballard's upstairs room. That was probably where he was. A few minutes later she saw him, pacing back and forth. Then he came to the window and stood there, his back to the light so she could not see his face.

As she had told Worden, she knew George Ballard better than anyone else in Gunlock, certainly better than Ellen who had seen only one side of him, his company side. She knew his cowardice and his inherent weakness; he had told her the scorching, bitter things old Longhorn Ballard had said to him when he was growing up.

Once in a moment of self-pity, he had said that if his grandfather had outlived his father, the Lazy B would have been willed to Jiggs Larribee. The old man had openly sneered at the bank. The ranch had been his life, and he had seen in Larribee the qualities he admired. That was part of George Ballard's trouble. Larribee, honest and loyal, had no real respect for George, and that hurt.

But George had inherited one Ballard quality. He was proud. He hated his grandfather, but at the same time he had been proud of the old man. He was proud of his father who had started the bank; he was proud of the Ballard name and what it stood for. And he was proud of the fortune his grandfather and father had made.

He turned from the window and began his pacing again. Nan, watching from behind the cast-iron deer, guessed what was going through his mind. It was the old conflict between his pride and his cowardice. He was afraid to buckle a gun around him and fight Worden the way old Longhorn would have done, but he could not overlook the injury he had received at Bill Worden's hands.

Now there was only one way to reconcile the fear and the wounded pride. He would shoot Worden from ambush. Nan had been certain that was what he would do when Worden had told her about his fight with George. The question was when and how he would try. She thought it would be in the morning, for he would have no chance tonight.

She waited through the cold hours, so chilled she shivered, the damp air working into her body; then she was aware that daylight was at hand, that the stars were fading and the eastern sky was beginning to glow with the coming dawn. The front door opened and Ballard came out. Before he closed the door, she caught a glimpse of the rifle in his hands.

He passed within twenty feet of her. A crazy temptation to shoot him struck her, but she knew at once that would be wrong. Even Worden would call it murder. No, she had to wait until there was no doubt of his intentions. Walking softly, far enough behind so he wouldn't see her, she followed him through the sleeping town.

Once she lost him in the darkness and she had to hurry. She was afraid he would hear her, but he had no reason to think anyone was following him and he had his mind fixed on what was ahead. He kept on, walking at a rapid pace, and she had to run to keep the same distance between them.

Before he reached Main Street, he turned up an alley. Again she had to hurry, for it was very dark here behind the row of buildings. He crossed a side street and went into another alley, and suddenly he disappeared.

She went on to the end of the alley, then realized that these buildings, mostly sheds and empty dwellings, all fronted on the street that ran along the north side of the courthouse square.

Carefully she retraced her steps, certain that he had gone into one of the buildings. The back doors were locked on most of them, but one was open, a shed that belonged to Luke Prentice who owned the feed store. He used it for storage, hay in the mow, and sacks of corn, wheat, bran, shorts, and other feeds on the first floor.

She slipped inside and stood with her back to the wall. She saw him a moment later, silhouetted against a front window. Suddenly he turned and walked directly to her. She froze there, holding her breath, her right hand on the gun in her pocket. But apparently he did not see her, for he climbed the ladder to the mow.

For a long moment she stood motionless, sick with the fear that he might have known she was following him and had seen her come in. Dark as it was, it was possible he had caught the blur of movement when she had slipped into the shed from the alley.

At this time of year the mow was nearly empty. She heard the boards squeak under his feet as he walked heavily to the street end. She knew then what he planned to do. There was a big door through which hay was forked into the mow, later to be forked back into customers' hayracks that could be pulled directly under the door.

Ballard would have a perfect view of the hanging. Shooting Worden from there would be easy enough, and in the excitement of the hanging, it was improbable that anyone would notice where the shot came from. Ballard would escape in the confusion. Once gone, there would be no proof against him.

She had to get up into the mow. But how? The slightest noise would attract his attention. She thought of going after Worden or McNamara. But Ballard had committed no crime. He might have difficulty explaining his presence and why he had brought a rifle. Still he could take an attitude of defiance, refusing to explain anything and contending it was nobody's business why he was there. In any case, they would have nothing against him.

The more she thought about it, the more she was convinced that she had to get up there and hide until he was ready to shoot. Then she'd stop him. There was probably some hay in the back of the mow, enough to hide her if she could reach it without his knowing.

She climbed the ladder, slowly and carefully. Outside the light was fairly strong, making a bright glow against the big door, but here in the back it was quite dark. She couldn't see him. Probably he was standing against the wall at the edge of the door.

She pulled herself up two more rungs of the ladder and stepped onto the floor. And then she was aware of him, standing beside her. She screamed and grabbed for her gun, but she was too late. He brought the rifle barrel down across her head and she fell forward into absolute blackness.

It was bright day when she came to, the sunlight falling across her face. She could not remember for a time what had happened; she was aware only of a pounding headache; then Ballard's voice reached her.

"So you came around."

She was lying on her back, her hands and feet tied. She wiggled into the corner so she was out of the blinding sunlight. Ballard was on the other side of the door, his rifle in his hands, his eyes on her.

"You finally found a way to get even with me, didn't you? But it's going to be expensive, Nan. I can't leave you alive to testify against me." He paused, then added, "You were pretty smart, figuring out what I'd do. Or did you just follow me?"

"Yes."

"Then Worden must have told you what he did to me."

"Yes."

"Well, it doesn't make any difference. Two shots, one for him and one for you; then I'll get out of here."

She struggled against the ropes, but there was no slack. She rolled a quarter turn so she lay on her side. She thought she could feel the gun in her pocket, but it would do her no good if she couldn't get her hands free. It took only a moment to discover he had done a good job tying her.

She asked, "What time is it?"

"Won't be long."

He wasn't as nervous as she had thought he would be. Because there was nothing she could do but talk, she said, "You didn't want to lose Ellen. Is that why you hate Worden enough to kill him, or is it because he gave you a beating?"

"Both."

"You were always a little man, George, little and weak. That's why you wanted to marry into Worden's family. You thought some of his strength would rub off on you."

He had been peering through a crack between two boards. Now he wheeled toward her, his anger stirred. "That's enough, Nan," he said. "You understand. Enough?"

He wanted to kill her, but he could not afford a shot. As he turned back to the crack, a feeling of absolute hopelessness gripped her. She would never see Lew again, and she wondered why she had been foolish enough to get into a mess like this.

# *Chapter Eighteen*

**AT** eight forty-five Worden left the courthouse with Lake. Orval Jones and McNamara walked in front, both armed with Winchesters. John Harris kept step with the condemned man. Worden followed, his nerves more tense than ever, for even now within fifteen minutes of the final moment, he still had no way of knowing what the ranchers would do.

The farmers had moved in from the boardwalk surrounding the courthouse to make two solid lines that ran from the door to the gallows. Outside these lines and on the other side of the gallows was the crowd, mostly townspeople with a sprinkling of farmer women.

Lew Hogan was the only cowman in sight. He stood outside the farmer lines, restless eyes searching the crowd for Nan. He did not know what to do or where to look, but one thing was plain. He had no interest in what happened to Lake, no interest at all, and that, to Worden, was the strangest thing of many strange things that had happened during these frantic hours.

Lake was controlling himself better than Worden had expected. He was pale, and sweat was a shiny film on his face, but he moved along, not looking to either side, his shoulders back, his head held high. Worden, watching him, could not help wondering if he still expected to be rescued.

Then Worden realized his throat was dry. They might be hiding, Poling and Jiggs Larribee and the rest of the cowmen, hiding in the sheds and empty houses that fronted on the street to the north of the courthouse square.

But time was running out for them. Whatever they did could be nothing more than an empty gesture of defiance. They wouldn't do it, he told himself. He felt the tension build in him; he licked his lips and tasted the sweat that rolled down his face, and he told himself he was crazy to keep on assuring himself that nothing would happen now. He didn't know. There would be twenty of them or more, and if they hit fast and hard in a sheet of gun-flame, anything could happen. He could see it all, the farmers running for cover, and himself and McNamara and Orval Jones shot down in the first volley. Again his eyes swept the sheds and empty houses, but he saw nothing that was not as it should be.

McNamara and Jones set a slow pace. They walked past Ben Smith and his sons, Harris and Lake keeping the same pace, and Worden behind them, past Orson and Rigdon and the others, stone-faced, grim men. Jones and McNamara reached the gallows and stepped aside, and Worden saw the reporters, Lesser and DeLong and the rest of them, the men who had built this case into something bigger

241

than it deserved to be.

Now they would see the last chapter; they would write about it, and the story would go out over the wire within the hour. They would dramatize it just as they had dramatized everything from the day Ed Lake had been arrested, but still they would miss much that would make good reading.

They would never know how Worden had bluffed and been tough when he'd had to be, had side-stepped and feinted and struck out like a skilled boxer, had worried through the eternal hours, made afraid by the uncertainty, fear he would never tell anyone.

They would not know about Rigdon, about Ryman who had turned against Lake after spending most of the night in jail with him, about Jeannie who would be waiting in Santa Fe for Lake, about Lew Hogan who had been driven frantic by his concern for Nan. And they would not know about Ellen and George Ballard.

All this was in Worden's mind, but only for an instant; then Doc Quinn joined him, and they climbed to the gallows behind Lake and Harris, Jones and McNamara following. Almost nine now, the sun hot and glaring upon the steaming earth.

Worden's eyes swept the crowd. Men like Tad Barton and Luke Prentice, their wives and children, come to see a free, ghastly show. Again anger was in him. Sordid, sadistic, a terrible thing that should not be happening, but he was powerless to prevent it.

McNamara tied Lake's hands and feet and fitted the noose around his neck. Worden asked, "Is there anything you want to say, Lake?"

The man's chin quivered. His eyes sought and found Hogan, and he turned back to Worden. "I never gave an employer away in my life, and I won't now."

So there it was, the answer to the question that had been in Worden's mind for a long time. Lake was a killer, without conscience, without scruples, and yet he had his private code of honor which prevented him from naming the man who had hired him.

Until this final moment Lake had clung to a desperate hope he would be rescued, but now he had no hope. Worden saw that, and he wondered if Lake felt any regret, any sympathy for the families of the men he had killed.

John Harris lifted a hand and prayed, asking God's forgiveness for this man if God, with His great mercy and wisdom, could forgive such a man. In the middle of the prayer Lake shouted, "Let her rip."

Lake's head was the only one that was not bowed. When Harris finished, Worden glanced at the farmers, and he saw the look on Rigdon's face, the wildness and the pleasure, and Worden thought, *He wants to be up here. He wants to spring the trap.*

McNamara fitted the black hood over Lake's

head and stepped aside. Worden glanced at his watch. Just a few seconds before nine. Once more he looked out over the crowd, then his gaze ran along the sheds and buildings to the north. Too late, he thought, too late for anything to happen.

The trap was sprung. Lake fell, and the rope snapped taut, quivering with the man's full weight upon it, his head twisted grotesquely. A strange sound was wrung from the crowd, a long, drawn-out sigh. So it was done, and then it came to Worden that he had never really expected it, that he had thought the night would never end, this moment would never come.

The sigh of the crowd was gone. No sound for a time, the glaring sunlight upon all of them, no movement but the swaying of the body, then a rifle cracked, and splinters flew from the frame of the gallows above Worden's head.

A scream rose from the crowd as it scattered. Some of the farmers at the far end of the line broke and ran, and Orval Jones threw down his Winchester and jumped off the platform to the grass. He started to get up and fell back, holding his ankle.

No one knew who had fired the shot or where it had come from. McNamara picked up his Winchester, shouting, "Anyone see who fired that shot?"

Worden drew his revolver, knowing the shot had been aimed at him and fully expecting another any second. He was not afraid, and that was queer, for he had been afraid during the night when he had waited for the attack that had never come.

Worden stared at the buildings north of the courthouse square because the thought had been in his mind a moment before that if the cattlemen were in town, that was where they would hide. He saw a man spill out of the big hay door of Prentice's shed, a rifle in his hands, saw him turn in the air and hit the ground on his head and shoulders a few feet in front of a wagon.

Ballard! Worden remembered what Nan had said, that Ballard would try to kill him, but Worden would not know when he tried. McNamara was the first man off the gallows' platform, but Worden remained with Doc Quinn and John Harris.

Hogan was out there, running beside McNamara toward Ballard. Judge Webb was behind them, and some of the farmers. Now the townsmen, Prentice and Barton and several others, recovering from their panic, were racing toward the shed. And on the ground Orval Jones cursed in pain as he tried to put his weight on his sprained ankle and toppled forward.

Worden did not go to where Ballard lay until Doc Quinn at nine:twelve pronounced Lake dead. When he reached the shed with the doctor, he stood beside Ballard's body while Quinn made his examination.

"His neck's broken," Quinn said as he rose. "Looks to me like it struck that wagon tongue."

The crowd had pushed into the shed. Now McNamara raged at the men. "Get back. This is the sheriff's business."

Worden went inside, the crowd opening a lane for him. He was cold. It was warm here inside the shed, and he blinked in the thin light. The coldness was inside him, a coldness that could not be touched by heat. He had the weird feeling he was walking beside himself, that some other power not his own was propelling him toward the rear of the shed.

"It's Nan Hogan," McNamara called. "She wants to see you."

George Ballard was dead! Worden shook his head and wiped a hand across his face. Ellen — how would she feel about this? What would she do? Why was it that women were the ones who were hurt? Like Jeannie Mason. Then he stood before Nan who was leaning against the wall, Lew's arm around her.

"She was tied like a calf ready for branding," McNamara said. "She won't talk to anybody but you. I'll run everyone out . . ."

"No, I just didn't want to tell it twice," Nan said.

She was very pale, her wrists raw where she had fought the ropes. Somehow she had saved Worden's life. He said, "You warned me."

The moment of shock had passed. He listened carefully to what Nan told him. She finished with, "I couldn't keep him from firing that one shot. All I could do was to wiggle along like a measuring worm. I knew he missed because he swore like he was crazy. He took quite awhile aiming. By that time I was close enough to raise my feet and kick him. He was standing right by the door. He just went on out."

Worden reached out and took her hands. He said, "Thanks, Nan."

It was all he could say, all he needed to say, and he saw the eagerness bring a glow to her face; he heard her breathless question, "Is it all right, Sheriff? About me? And Lew?"

"It's all right," Worden said, "only next time, Lew, you listen to your wife."

Worden went outside. Men were waiting to shake his hand and pat him on the back. Somehow he got away from them. He brushed the reporters aside. Then, when he reached the courthouse door, he found John Harris waiting.

"You haven't heard, I guess," Harris said, "but when you were in Prentice's shed, the cowmen showed up. Larribee and Poling were leading them. As soon as they saw that Lake was already hanged, they turned around and rode back. You know, Sheriff, a man's pride is a strange thing. They didn't really want to fight to save Lake, but they thought they had to."

Worden nodded, thinking that was true, but he was thinking, too, that only a matter of minutes, perhaps seconds, had made the difference between a peaceful hanging and a fight that would have meant the death of many men. Pride, yes, but an honest pride and a conviction that Ballard had lacked.

Harris held out his hand. "I'm glad we have you for our sheriff, Mr. Worden."

"Thank you," Worden said, and climbed the stairs to his office. On his desk lay the letter addressed to Jeannie Mason. Impulsively he tore it open and read the scrawled lines.

"You've got my money, you damned bitch. You'll be living high as long as it lasts, but you might as well know I never loved you. I used you because you were cheap."

Without even considering whether he had a right to destroy the letter, Worden struck a match and burned it. Jeannie was far away, but wherever she was, she would not lose the illusion of love. It was her right to keep it, but it was different with Ellen.

He rose and left the courthouse. He had to know. Everything would be all right with Ada. And Kirby when he heard what had happened. But Ellen? He walked past men, not seeing them, and they did not speak when they saw his face.

He climbed the hill to his house, thinking that at last he could relax. He could sleep the clock around, and he wondered if he would ever be rested again. Then he thought about the town, of the men who had given him no help, hangers-on who wanted protection from the law but who gave nothing to make the law mean something. The ranchers who had made one final, futile effort, and then turned back when they saw they were too late, defeated men who would soon leave the valley, most of them, for now none of them could deny the future. And the farmers to whom that future belonged, the only ones who had backed the law.

Ada saw him coming. She ran down the steps to him and he put his arms around her and held her so hard it was difficult for her to breathe. She whispered, "You're all right, Bill?"

"Sure I'm all right. You shouldn't have worried."

"I know, I know."

She tipped her head back and looked at him, and he thought how much he loved her, how important she had been to him through these years when he had ridden into danger so often. She whispered, "I'm proud of you, Bill, so proud. If anyone else had been sheriff, a lot of men would have been killed this morning."

He realized then that she understood much more about him than he had guessed, known and trusted and taken pride in him. He kissed her, and tears ran down her cheeks and she was unashamed.

He asked, "Does Ellen know about Ballard?"

Ada nodded. "Mrs. Webb stopped by and told us. Go upstairs and talk to Ellen."

They went into the house together. He took off his hat and gunbelt and laid them down; he looked around the room at the worn furniture. It was enough. Why should he question happiness?

He found Ellen standing by the window in her

room, straight-backed and proud. She had been crying, but she wasn't now, and when she heard him come in, she turned and ran to him.

He said, "I'm sorry . . ."

She put a hand against his mouth. "Don't be sorry about anything, Daddy. Just give me a little time." She stopped, her face upturned to his, and he thought as he had so many times that she was the image of her mother. Then she said, "Something happened to me last night. I don't know . . ."

She couldn't finish. She didn't really know, he thought, not yet, but she would later. She would not let this thing destroy her future. She was his daughter, his and Ada's, and for the first time in years he felt there was no gap between them.

"I've been thinking," she said finally. "Kirby wants to go to school. It wouldn't be so expensive if I went, too, and we got an apartment and I kept house for him. Kirby's saving his money. Do you think we could manage it?"

He had planned that very thing for them, and he and Ada had talked about it before Ellen had taken Ballard's ring. He would not be able to buy some things Ada needed, but that would be a small price to pay.

"Yes," he said, "I'm sure we can manage it."

The employees of G.K. Hall hope you have enjoyed this Large Print book. All our Large Print titles are designed for easy reading, and all our books are made to last. Other G.K. Hall books are available at your library, through selected bookstores, or directly from us.

For information about titles, please call:

(800) 223-1244
(800) 223-6121
To share your comments, please write:

Publisher
G.K. Hall & Co.
P.O. Box 159
Thorndike, ME  04986

W